STEELFLOWER IN SNOW

LILITH SAINTCROW

STEELFLOWER IN SNOW Copyright © 2017 by Lilith Saintcrow

Cover art copyright © 2018 by Skyla Dawn Cameron

Trade Paperback ISBN: 9780999201312

Mass Market Paperback ISBN: 9780999201381

STEELFLOWER IN SNOW

For Skyla Dawn Cameron.
Because without her, it wouldn't be.

CERTAIN PROPRIETIES

IT BEGAN TO DRIZZLE, *a chill dispirited prickle-rain Clau sailors call moonbreath, for they believe her the source of all cold as the sun is all heat. I hunched, watching the paved expanse of the North Road from the shelter of a cranyon tree's bulk, its branches not yet naked but full of vibrant-painted, dying leaves. Antai simmered in its cup, down to the liquid glitter of the harbour, smoke-haze frothing like the foam on well-whisked chai. The ponies—shaggy beasts with wise eyes and mischievous dispositions—were much smaller than any I would have selected. Red-fist, however, pronounced them the best choice for the North in this season. There were no Skaialan draft horses in the markets; the farmers in the hinterlands prizing them too highly to send them down into the bowl. Our red bar-barian giant was too big for the ponies, but his legs had carried him from Hain to a battlefield, then back to Vulfentown and over the sea. Once we were through the Pass, he said, he could find a mount if he wished.*

A little further up the Road, well out of even crossbow range, a slatternly tavern leaned upon its exhausted stable. It was slightly flea-bitten, but safe enough for Redfist to sit with a tankard for a while. A few hours along the road was the furthest I had gone in that particular direction.

Just as the Danhai plains were the furthest west I'd gone from the Rim. I was too exhausted to suppress the shudder that always went through me when I dwelled too long upon those two years.

Even through the chill mist, I could sense the heat of approaching murder. I stepped away from the tree, my dotani ringing from its sheath. We were lucky the commission had not been high enough to interest a daykiller. Those are almost impossible to halt, and their price reflects as much.

No, this black Dunkast perhaps did not understand Antai's Guild, or there was a reason he wished Redfist murdered in the dark. He had paid in pale Northern gold, not the good ruddy gloss of Shainakh Rams, or so the smoking, stinking, reeking wreck of an assassin had told me. The hand that had carried the gold was none other than Corran Ninefinger's; the blond giant could have been simply a stupid catspaw. Soon enough they would hunt him down, too, if they had not already. Redfist did not say what had prompted his blond fellow giant to come south.

Put your worries away, Kaia. They are not needed here.

I took my position in the middle of the North Road. Later, mud would creep across the stones in slow rivers, and here above the bowl, away from the harbor's breath, it would freeze. A pale cloud puffed out of my mouth, drops of water flashing through it, and the shadows moved on the other side of the crumbling arc of walls that had been witchery-strong in the Pensari's day. It had been a long while since the great city had needed its shell upon the hilltops.

Dusky rainlight turned them into cloak-wrapped enigmas, kerchiefs over their mouths, their hoods dripping with the moisture. Hands folded inside wide sleeves, three of the Guild eyed me. I returned the favor.

One of them would be a representative of the clan who

had sent last night's courtiers. One would be sent directly from the Head and the Council, to make certain proprieties were observed. The third would be a witness from another clan, one most likely not allied with the first. No doubt I would have to pay double-dues next tithing-season —if I returned. The commission was bound to have a provision for interference, and hopefully it was not large enough to tempt anyone outside the walls with winter fast approaching.

We eyed each other, and I tensed, my *dotani* rising slightly. Scuffling sounds, high fast breathing, and movement behind them. Two shadows, with a third held awkwardly between them.

They held thiefcatchers, long wooden spars age-darkened and banded with iron. Each had a prong, like a *yueh* rune that had lost half a leg to battleground injury; the shorter half ended in a *hocta*-knot around the prisoner's neck, the spare loop snugged under the armpits. The longer was attached to the girdle, and walking inside that contraption was unsteady at best and bloody at worst.

They call it the Chastity, for the short spikes on the inside.

She was forced to her knees before the three senior Guild members, and a muffled curse told me who it was. A chill spread over me.

Even if I forgave Sorche Smahua's-kin, there was still this to face. If fate had been kinder, she might have chosen a sellsword's path instead of a thief's clan, or had it chosen for her. Even if the first assassin had taken it upon herself to avenge Sorche's thiefmother, the Sorche as the elder should have restrained her. Not only had she robbed the clan of the investment her little thiefling had represented, but the clumsiness of said little thiefling had warned me to be wary and perhaps cost the Smoke—or another clan— part of a fat commission.

It was not the potential death of a Guild member in

good standing they would punish her for. It was the loss of profit. There are many temples in Antai, many gods from both the hinterlands and abroad, but the one who rules beneath, above, and throughout them all had been disobeyed, and would take due vengeance.

One of the elders moved forward. A murmur was probably the delivery of the sentence in old Pensari, and a long silence showed where that word, the one that was never uttered, fit into its contours. The sibilants carried, and a breeze shook the cranyon tree's leaves. A rattle as some fell, the wet gleam of a blade.

"Mother!" Sorche cried, just before the most senior clanmember, the one in the middle, wrenched her head back. She might have fought, too, but the other two had her arms and the thiefcatchers were braced. A high spattering jet of arterial blood as her throat was opened, and I did not look away.

Some are children for their entire lives. Hot, rancid fluid boiled in my throat. There was no chai that would wash away the taste.

They watched as I strode for the wall-line; I felt a burst of concern—D'ri, wedged in the cranyon tree's upper reaches with his bow—as I moved forward and into bow-range from the crumbling stone. My left hand moved for a pocket, and I halted just on the other side of the invisible boundary.

I held up the Shainakh red Ram, its shine visible even in this darkness. The Moon hid her face behind a passing cloud, and I flicked the gold off my fingers in the thieves' way, the metal describing a high spinning arc before a dark-gloved hand blurred out to catch it.

"For her pyre," I said, as clearly as I could, in tradespeak.

One nodded, a fractional dip of the muffled head. They could have thrown her body over the wall. This way, at least, her spirit would rise on the smoke and join her thiefmother's, in whatever afterworld the two of them might share.

I turned my back on them, but I did not sheathe my dotani. I walked, steadily, for the cranyon again, its bole a wet pillar and its outline blurring with moisture. The thin piercing rain had soaked into my braids; they were heavy once more, my neck throbbing with tension. My teeth ached as well—I forced myself to loosen my jaw, despite the risk of the bubble in my throat bursting.

If it did, I decided, I would swallow it.

AND THAT WAS how we left Antai.

FIRST SNOW

THE ROAD REMAINED EASY ENOUGH, though it began to climb on the third afternoon. Broad farmland on either side lay under a pall of mist for the first five days as we wended north and vaguely west from Antai, the Lan'ai Shairukh receding further with every step. Big red-furred Rainak Redfist did not speak much, striding all day with uncomplaining and deceptive placidity. His bearded chin jutted thoughtfully, and the beads braided into his face-pelt clicked every so often. When we stopped at waystations he did more than his share, as if in apology for the disruption to our plans.

Darik rode silently, and the ponies liked him a great deal. He had already begun preparing their hooves for ice, teaching them to be familiar with his touch.

And I? I found myself thinking much upon the past. Uncomfortable, certainly, and never to be recommended unless one is longing to learn a lesson or two from experience. Even then, it is always better to look forward.

There was no minstrel-strumming at our nightly fire, no child to chatter or sing Vulfentown drinking-songs in a high sweet unbroken voice, none of Janaire's soft merriment or Atyarik's easy companionship with another *s'tarei*. I had grown...accustomed to our little troupe, as I had to few others during my travels. Perhaps it was merely a measure of how long we had endured each others' company.

At least they were safe in Antai. They would spend the winter there in something like comfort, and spring would see our reunion, if all went well.

I did not think it would, but what else could I do? I had given my word, and Redfist could not go alone. Not after I had spent so much effort keeping his flour-pale hide in one piece since picking his pocket in a Hain tavern.

Traveling-calm descended upon our trio. Redfist often hummed Skaialan melodies, his swinging strides marking the rhythm; on the second day I began to hum as well, a wandering counterpoint that sometimes slid through remembered childhood songs. D'ri was content to listen, scanning the far horizon with a line between his coal-black eyebrows. Whether he expected trouble or was simply lost in his thoughts, I did not ask.

Instead, our talk was all of commonplaces—the ponies, where to rest, the likelihood of the mist or the rain breaking in the afternoon, what piece of gear needed repairing or modification. The towns became villages with hostels instead of inns; the taverns became smaller and quieter. For days the blue smear of mountains on the northern horizon came no closer. It was late in the season for caravans to start, but we found evidence of their passing everywhere, especially in the waystations where the firewood was restocked and the straw full of still-green fislaine to keep the mice away.

The Road went only halfway through the Pass,

they said, and after that you were left to forge your way without Pensari poured stone underfoot. Even the Pensari did not encroach further upon the Highlands, and it cannot have been because of the ice alone; the giants of the north are held to be fierce and unruly. I found Redfist tractable enough, though I could well imagine how an entire room of ale-loving, bearded mountains might cause concern to smaller folk.

Not to mention the smell, if they were as ripe as Corran Ninefinger, or Redfist himself when I found him.

It was almost a moonturn before the sharptooth mountains drew close enough to oppress and the Road began to rise more sharply. The house-roofs rose as well, peaks meant to slide rain and snow away like a courtesan's robe down his shoulders. The hinterland folk are closemouth and drive hard bargains, but they are honorable enough when travelers mind their *own* mouths and manners. They call that mountain range *Amath-khalir*, an ancient conjunction that means rocks which do not lose their snow in summer.

No doubt the Pensari had other names for it.

We made good time, with the ease of sellswords used to long journeys. At least we had not been in Antai long enough to soften. Sometimes we continued half the night, relying on Redfist's memory of the hamlets and their contents along the ribbon of Pensari stonework. Their roads were not the broad curving avenues of the Hain or the flat-cobbled Shainakh streets; no, everywhere the Pensari ruled the crossroads are spokes of a wheel and the ribbon-roads straight as could be, only barely altering course a degree or two for some stubborn knot in the landscape. Most of the time, they slice straight through such silly things as hills, or leap across torrents with their sturdy poured-stone bridges the Antai have lost the secret of making. There are stories of folk who may make stone live and grow as green things do, but I have never traveled far enough to see *that* witchery. In G'maihallan, such a thing could be done, but would perhaps be considered tasteless, and a waste of Power besides.

The frosts came, and soon enough the ground hardened. Carts on the road, heaped high with fodder or late produce, became fewer. The travelers we met were all streaming south, and no few of them must have laughed at the fools traveling in the opposite direction at that season. Then there were no carts and precious few travelers for a day or so, and the bite to the wind brought a rosiness to what little of Redfist's cheeks could be seen under red fur.

"Strange," I remarked at a nooning, as the ponies drank their fill from a clear, cold, fast-running streamlet already rimed at its edges. "There are no Skaialan traveling this road."

Redfist, scrubbing at his face and the back of his neck with a rag from my clothpurse, gave a short bark of amusement. "Noticed that, did ye?"

I glanced at D'ri. His hair, neatly trimmed in the Anjalismir *s'tarei* style I remembered from my youth, was wind-mussed, and he looked as if he enjoyed the chill. At least it was not a heaving deck, and we had no disagreements to speak of.

"Is it usually otherwise?" my *s'tarei* asked.

"In this season? Those who can get through the Pass might not be able to return, but there's always a few." Redfist sounded grim. "Karnagh's probably closed tighter than a miser's wife-basket, though. Corran gave a hint or two."

"Did he." *And when were you going to share the hints*

with me, barbarian? I stroked the red-and-white pony's neck, enjoying the texture. Gloves and furs would soon be necessary, but at least the *taih'adai* had taught me of the warming breath and a few other ways to keep ice from a G'mai. The nightly lighting of the fire without sparkstones had mixed results—either I could barely produce an anemic flame, or the pile of tinder evaporated into ash after a ball of hungry orange fury devoured it wholesale. Still, I generally managed to call a fire into being without singing a roof or either of my companions, and that was well enough.

"Never thought it would come to this." A heavy sigh bowed Redfist's wide shoulders. He ceased at his scrubbing, looking at the mountains as if they held an answer to some riddle not yet voiced. "He was a cousin. Knew his father."

"He may not have known everything in the commission." I ran my fingers through thickening horse-fur, the vital haze of heat and life from the pony all but visible. Every living thing cloaked itself in that trembling energy, Power begging to be tapped, released, shaped into harmony and brilliance. A continual wonder; how did other *adai* deal with the distraction? "But he did deliver it to the Guild."

"How much?" Redfist dropped his blue gaze to the rag of Hain cotton, working it around his callused fingers.

It had taken him a long time to ask. There was no reason not to tell him. "Two hundred pieces of pale Northern gold, each stamped with a wolfshead sigil." *A princely sum, indeed.* The Guild would not scruple to return it unless the commission was withdrawn, either, so our barbarian could not return to Antai just yet.

"So. At least I am worth something." Redfist

paused. "And new coinage. The mines…" A shake of his head, his red hair pulled back and tied in a club with a leather thong. "Tis a fool's errand, this. The Pass may well be closed."

"Do you wish to turn back?" I turned my gaze away, in case he could not admit it while watched. The trees had changed; instead of those who disrobed every autumn, those who drew their green finery higher against the cold surrounded us. They are secretive, those dark masses, and their pungency can fill the head just like mead.

"Aye." He wrung the rag with a quick, brutal twist. "Of course I do. But I cannot."

Fair enough. There are many things in life a sellsword would turn away from, if she could.

"What else will I do with my life?" he continued, shaking the poor piece of cloth viciously. "Sellsword until I am too old, then beg upon a street?"

"I plan on opening an inn." It was out before I could halt my babbling. "Six rooms, waterclosets to match, hanging linens in the sun and foxing tax collectors."

The silence was deafening. Even the noise of a forest—creaking, birdsong, the vast echoing of the sky-roof itself—hushed for a few moments, as if the trees and fauna were likewise drawing breath to laugh at my folly.

Redfist threw his head back and laughed, too. It was not *quite* the reaction I had expected, but then, nobody expects to lay one of their cherished dreams before another. Not comfortably, at least. Who wishes to show their own foolishness, even to a drinking-companion, let alone a friend?

"Lass," Redfist finally said, chuckles still burbling in his gut, "ye're the wisest sellsword I ever hae known. I thank my gods ye picked my pocket that night."

It was kind of him to say so. He may even have meant it, and I found myself smiling. "'Tis not much of a dream."

"I like it," D'ri said, smoothing the other pony's mane much as I had. His lips had curved and his gaze softened, and it suited him well indeed. "It seems an honest thing, and a gentle one."

"I am not sure of either." I shifted my attention to the horizon, a collection of white linen hoods on marching heads like devotees of Taryina-Ak-Allat during their great ecstatic festivals, threading through spiraling streets and chanting atonal songs of sacrifice. "'Tis more likely I shall end with three rooms and a single watercloset, or gut-pierced on a battlefield."

"Not while your *s'tarei* lives, Kaia." Darik's words were edged but very soft, G'mai rolling with consonants providing sharp peaks to match those I watched.

I did not have a chance to reply, for Redfist folded the rag and tucked it in his belt to dry. "I shall nae stand to see *that* happen, lass. Come, we waste sunlight." As if *he* had not been the one to suggest a nooning.

THAT NIGHT, the first snow fell, and I began to dream.

WE SHALL MEET IT

I CHARGED. *Not straight for my opponents, though that would have been satisfying, but to the left, where the shadows were deepest. Boots stamping, my legs complaining, ice underfoot, my left knee threatened to buckle again before silence descended upon me. It was not the killing snow-quiet I had discovered after my mother's death but the white-hot clarity of battlerage. There is a moment, when the body has been pushed past endurance and your enemies are still all about you, when the last reserves inside a sellsword—those crockery jars full of burn-the-mouth, sweetheavy* turit *jam—are smashed. Muscle may pull from bone, bone itself may break, but the sellsword will not feel either for hours. The Shainakh call it* nahrappan, *the Hain a term that has to do with a cornered animal, and in G'mai it is called the s'tarei's last kiss, and it is said that even after an adai's death a s'tarei may perform one final action, laying waste to his opponents.*

The Skaialan call it berserk, *and there are tales of their warriors fighting naked except for crimson chalk-paint, touched by their chieftain-god Kroth's heavy hand and driven mad by the weight.*

Pain vanished. My dotani *clove frozen air with a sweet sound, blurring in a low arc as I turned sideways, skipping from cobble to cobble with no grace but a great deal of speed. The far-left Black Brother had an axe, and all thought left me as it moved, hefted as if it weighed less than a straw. Their soft, collective, invisible grasping burned away; I left the ground and flew, turning at the last moment, my* dotani's *arc halting and cutting down, sinking through fur and leather, snap-grinding on bone, and the Black Brother's mouth opened wet-loose as his arm separated, neatly cloven. The axe, its momentum inescapable, sheared to the side, and since his left hand was the brace for the haft it arced neatly into his next-door compatriot, sinking in with the heavy sound of well-seasoned wood.*

Child-high screams rose, but I was already past and Mother Moon, I longed to turn back. The burning in my veins, the sweet-hot rage, demanded it.

Instead, I put my head down and bolted, braids bouncing and my joints aching with each foot-stamp. Thump-thud, thump-thud, the street familiar now, each shadow turning bright-sharp as my pupils swelled, the taste in my mouth sour copper and katai *candy. The Keep loomed ever closer, and if I could reach the end there was a narrow housefront with a door left deliberately unlocked. Once inside, I could be up the stairs and out a high window, onto the roof-road again, up and down while their foulglove net closed on empty air. There was an easy way into the Keep from there, if D'ri had reached it and secured the knotted rope...*

A whistle-crunch. Another high childlike cry behind me as a heavy black-fletched arrow, its curve aimed high and sharp to give it added force as it fell, pierced a pursuer's skull, shattering it in a spray of bone and grey matter.

Kaia! *Thin and very far away, Darik struggling to reach me through the rage.* Kaia, down!

∾

"KAIA." A hand at my shoulder, a short sharp shake. My hand flung out as if to ward off a blow—Darik caught my wrist, cold, calloused fingers strong but not biting. I had not reached for the knife under the almost-empty bag of fodder serving as my pillow, so I must have known it was him even in unconsciousness.

Redfist's snores echoed against the waystation's walls. D'ri must have been on watch. His grasp gentled and he touched my forehead with his other hand, as if he suspected an *adai*'s fever had me in its grip. "All is well," he said, softly. "You were dreaming."

"Was I?" The change from bright dream-daylight to the darkness inside a small waystation—the last stone cube meant for travelers on this side of the Pass, Redfist said—threatened to blind me. I could not find enough air, and a touch of sweat along my nape sent a thin finger of chill all down my back.

"It sounded very much like it." D'ri crouched, easily, and as my nightvision returned I caught the gleam of his dark eyes under a shelf of blueblack hair. "The one from the ship?"

I reclaimed my hand, rubbed at the solid sleep crusting my eyelids. At least they were not frozen shut; thin threads of crimson on the banked fire were more a suggestion than actual heat or light. "Again," I muttered into my palms. "The same thing, all the time." My Anjalismir accent had grown more pronounced when I spoke to him of late. Sometimes it did not even cause a pang to hear his tender inflection—or my own.

"Ah." He glanced at the waystation door, firmly shut and barred. Shuttered arrow-slits piercing the walls were covered with horse-blankets, to muffle the sting of night chill; the ponies moved restlessly and the fragrance of their hides and breath—not to mention other, nastier odors—had vanished from conscious attention, we spent so long breathing them.

You do not allow your beasts to sleep outside this far north. The white winds can come without warning, and there are stories of livestock frozen stiff near the Pass when the blind storms descend.

"Will you tell me?" Uncertain, as if he expected me to take offense at the question.

No. Perhaps. "Tis nothing. Merely dreams." I used the word for idle thoughts, things best put aside. Now I could see his expression, and a flash of something crossed his face. Was it pain? He nodded, sharply, and would have risen had I not caught at his sleeve. "D'ri..." The words trembled on my tongue. *They keep returning, and I think I saw Rikyat die in one of them, but...*

How many years had it been since I turned to anyone for...comfort? Was that what I wanted?

He waited. A hot, abrupt bite of shame pierced my chest. He was, after all, a very patient *s'tarei*, even among my kind.

"They bother me," I finally admitted, in a whisper. "I think...I think they may be *an'farahl'adai*."

He sank down, no longer crouching but sitting, The black silk and leather of a G'mai princeling was hidden under thick woolens, and if not for the tips of his ears or the severe Dragaemir beauty of his features, he might have been another sellsword, a comrade of convenience along the Road. "Not future-knowing, but otherwise." Reminding himself what it meant—the ways of Power are many and strange, and only a Yada'Adais can lay claim to knowing most their manifestations.

Nobody knows all ways but the Moon, as the proverb runs, *for she is mistress of all hidden and secret places.*

"I think...there was one, I think I saw how Rikyat died." My throat was dry, but leaving my sleeping-pad and nest of blankets to fetch a drinking-skin was a daunting proposition, even in woolen night-boots and carrying blankets with me. "And this one, you are in it, and the giant, Janaire and Atyarik too."

"At least they are safe in the city." A vertical line appeared between his eyebrows, and he made no further move to retreat. "If it is your Power breaking free, you may have visions. Like Janaire."

"I hope not." A shudder worked through me—before the battle with the Hamashaiiken, Janaire had *seen*. She did not speak much of it, but any G'mai child knows such a 'gift' is a burden and a weight upon the soul.

"It could be a temporary symptom." His palm against my cheek, warm though his fingers were cool. "I cannot guess, I am no Yada'Adais."

"Nor am I." *I have left my Teacher behind.* Janaire's cooking would have been welcome on our path, and Atyarik's help with ponies and the work of making camp. I did not precisely *miss* them—or did I? It was a comfort to think of them warm and snug in the Antai residence, bundled against a cold ameliorated by the breath of the Lan'ai.

Darik's thumb feathered over my cheekbone. "Fear not, *adai'mi*. However the Power moves, we shall meet it."

Too fine for me by far, my *s'tarei*. The weight lifted from my shoulders, and I would have taken the rest of his watch, but he tucked me into my nest afresh and pressed his lips to my forehead, and I let him. If I dreamed again that night, I did not remember it.

THE EATER

THE PASS HAS A LOVELY NAME—*ARMARA-KARNHA*. The sound is pleasing and balanced, but the meaning is altogether different. Like any place that had ever heard of the Pensari, whiteness along the northern mountains of the Rim is suspect at best and murderous at worst, and the name means *the White Eater*. The crags are knifelike, massive teeth of some world-breaking beast; wind constantly sliding along their edges in a low moaning rising to a shriek as clouds from the south freeze and fall. There are pillars of ice in the higher reaches that have never melted since the world's creation, and stories tell of wind-spirits trapped in those long cloudy daggers, endlessly suffocating.

"*Get down!*" Darik barked, and I did not hesitate, throwing myself full-length into a snowbank. Something whistled near my hair, its buffeting blew stinging snow and freezing over me; I rolled, floundering in a sea of cold white wet.

None know why harpies screech as they do, and their faces, gnarled into an expression of suffering, only add to the effect. Twin swellings on their feathered chests are full of venom, and their claws drip with it as they work, aching to drive into prey. They love meat, and will feast upon whatever they find, either freshly envenomed into quiescence or frozen carrion. Their sharp-feathered wings are broad, and powerful enough to knock a strong man down with their noisome breath. I have heard they can strip a brace of oxen to bone and offal in bare heartbeats, and I believe it very near the truth.

The thing shrieked as a finely fletched arrow buried itself just under the juncture of its left wing. Bright hot blood spattered, already half-frozen by the time it hit the snow around me. I flicked a boot up, smacking the thing's hindquarter to drive it aside as it fell, and its claws snapped a bare fingerwidth from my thigh.

"*Kaia!*" Redfist bellowed, and there was a glitter as a flung axe buried itself in the harpy's side just under the arrow. He almost clove the thing in half, and now I understood why he insisted one of us should always keep a watch overhead. It had come out of *nowhere*, and if not for my *s'tarei* I might have been reduced to mincemeat in a few moments.

Two more banked overhead, turning in great circles, their cries threadbare on the rising wind. Darik tore his arrow free of the corpse—the harpy was longer than I was, how could such a thing *fly*? My *s'tarei* offered a hand, I took it gladly, and he dragged me from the snow's wet clutching. The ponies rolled their eyes and cried out in fear, but fortunately did not bolt.

Perhaps they were intelligent enough to know there was no safety in fleeing down the Pass. Not in this weather.

Redfist did not seem to feel the cold; likely his

ruddy fur trapped the warmth next to his pale skin. D'ri and I both had the warming-breath now, but had Janaire not insisted upon training me, I might have frozen to death the night before we crested the Eater's throat and began sliding down the other side. It was upon that high spine the harpy finally decided I looked like easy prey, being the smallest creature braving the icy passage.

They would not have been able to lift either of my companions from the ground.

Darik brushed snow from my fur-lined cloak as Redfist tore his axe free from the steaming corpse, its eyes now filmed and its feathers scattered. There was a certain beauty to its gray and white plumage, and I could see how the marks on its bony cheeks and proud, vicious beak only resembled human features.

I had never thought I would see a harpy in the flesh. Especially so close.

We half stumbled, half slid down the slope, but the two circling overhead did not dive until we were well away. They settled on the body of their former comrade, and the clacking, whistling sounds of pleasure they made were enough to feature in many a nightmare.

"Tis a good thing our foster-son is safe," Darik muttered, while Redfist and I brushed the snow from his shoulders as well. My hood almost hid my face, and the tips of my ears were numb despite the warming-breath. "Those things could carry him aloft."

"No worse than wingwyrms." My heart pounded in my chest, and a thin trickle of melting ice slid down my neck. "I would kill for a hot bath right now."

"Better than a bath to be had, lass." The corners of Redfist's blue eyes crinkled merrily. His beard hung with ice, and every so often he would shake crackling bits of it free. "But not until Karnagh."

There was a rending of bone and a squabbling up the hill. I suppressed a flinch, squinting against snowglare. "Thank you, D'ri."

He nodded, pressed his lips to my forehead quickly. Redfist watched with a great deal of amusement, and clucked at the ponies, soothing them.

That night, we sheltered in a small cave, burrowing like animals. In the middle of my watch—I took the first—there was a rumbling in the heights; it shook both Redfist and D'ri awake.

"Kroth guard us all." The barbarian's tone was hushed, and he pushed himself up on one elbow from a small mount of furs and blankets next to the ponies, who were probably glad of his warmth. "The mountains are hungry tonight."

I shut my eyes, imagining ice, snow, rock tumbling down the side of those sheer slopes, gathering speed and weight, a wall of white death. "Avalanche," I said, quietly, in G'mai.

"I thought as much," D'ri answered. "Are they common here too, then?"

"Anywhere there are mountains, I suppose." I switched to tradespeak, pulling my cloak tighter around me. "He wishes to know if they are common," I translated politely, for Redfist's benefit. He could not seem to fit G'mai in his mouth.

It is a difficult language for those not born to it, not like trade-pidgin or Shainakh.

"Worst in spring, when the melt comes." Redfist flopped back down with a groan. The ponies stirred restlessly, one whickering to express his unease. "But aye, common enough."

"Luck." I made the *avert* sign with my left hand.

"Go back to sleep, I will wake you when your watch draws nigh."

A FIVEDAY LATER, we reached Karnagh.

THE DEATH GATE

THE CITY HOLDING the key to the Pass is a collection
of stone with red-tiled, sharply slanted roofs ready to
slough snow. And *noise*. Not to mention smell. Karnagh's size is shocking even against the mountains;
the buildings are stolid and massive under their
peaked dull-crimson caps. I barely reached Redfist's
chest, D'ri his shoulder, and the barbarian's countrymen are of like stature. Giants indeed, and all their
structures are built to their scale.

They dress strangely, as well—the men in woven,
full-sleeved shirts and long sheets of material folded
a certain way to provide cover and freedom of movement without the aid of trousers, the women in
longer skirts and furs. Their bearded men disdain the
cold; their hairy calves are on display above thick
boots and much-folded stockings held in place with a
buckle even in the worst of freezes. Outside the borders of their country, they walk. Inside, however,
their steeds are...different. I had thought we would
find Skaialan draft horses, and never understood
why Redfist laughed each time I mentioned them.
They breed the horses for export, and for the races
they bet furiously upon, but when a giant of the

North rides to war or to travel, he does so upon a *torkascraugh*, a creature I hesitate to describe, for even a bard might not believe me.

Torkascruagh appear squat only because their legs are columns of muscle, and their hooves are cloven. Their faces are long, and even the females sport two giant teeth, one on either side of a moist, flat muzzle. Their ears are tasseled, and they are shaggy enough to withstand even the white winds from the mountains.

In short, they appear as...well, giant *pigs*. Or, more precisely, boar, but even the Hain would not ride to hunt *those* tusked monstrosities.

We rode through a postern at the south edge of the city, next to the Death Gate—named thus because in winter nothing but Death rides through, or so they say. Those on watch inquired in their rough rolling tongue as to our business, and whatever Redfist said gained us entrance without even a token bit of copper tradewire spent. Indeed, they became respectful, both of them pale-haired, ice-crusted giants with massive flails. No doubt they could hold the postern against any southron invasion, and they peered at Darik and me with no little curiosity. What little of Redfist's tongue he had managed to teach me did not help much, though I could now ask for the location of the privy and three mugs of mead comfortably enough. I would have to soak myself in the city for a short while to gain more than a child's clumsy pointing and babble.

Inside, my first taste of Karnagh was the reek— wet stone, cold damp, the hot nastiness of some large animal's dung, a haze of smoke, unwashed bodies. My second was the sight of a *torkascraugh*, a bearded and well-furred figure clinging to its broad black back and shouting drunkenly as the beast's legs pumped so frantically they blurred. It was *quick*, for such a massive creature, and the onlooking crowds laughed as the rider blundered his way down a high, choking-narrow cobbled street. Redfist's coppery eyebrows rose and his laugh joined the others, a deep-welling thunder.

They laugh often and fight each other oftener, the men of the Highlands.

I glanced at D'ri, who frankly stared, that line between his eyebrows growing deeper. It was either a mark of perplexity or fastidiousness, but I could not decide which. In either case, Redfist cupped his hands and shouted something, and I looked along the walls and roofs with a thief's practiced eye and a sell-sword's consciousness of possible escape routes.

It did not look promising. The slopes looked too ice-crusted slippery for good thieving, even for one light and quick. Barred, solid shutters looked sturdy enough to keep both the cold and thieving climbers away. Perhaps it was a pickpocket's city, but such an operation requires anonymity, and good luck achieving such a state if you are surrounded by blunt-eared barbarians who apparently have never seen a copper-skinned face for long seasons.

Redfist turned, clapped D'ri on the shoulder with bruising force, a jolt I felt. "A good sign, that! Means the gods are with us. Come!" He set off with an entirely different gait—limber and loose, for once not hesitant as if the stones would crack underneath his big boots.

D'ri walked his pony, but I rode, and noted the sideways looks and hush of the crowd. The barbarian was not the stranger here. *We* were, my *s'tarei* and I.

The most dangerous time in a city are the first few days, before you learn the rhythm of cart-and-

foot traffic, the subtle shadows of its alleys, the un-
spoken rules of tavern and bath-house.

Of course, Redfist had intimated there were no
such things as bath-houses in his homeland. I suppressed a curse and Darik caught at my pony's reins
as well, obviously meaning to lead me as a *s'tarei*
would any *adai* a-horse on a crowded thoroughfare. I
set my jaw and let him, though I would have much
preferred to steer my own course in Redfist's wake.
Karnagh swallowed us; we had achieved the
Highlands.

Behind us, the Road was nigh impassable. Or so
we thought, then.

NOT SOMETHING I WISH TO
PROPAGATE

"No BATHS," I repeated, for it beggared belief. I had not believed him before now, thinking it a jest. *"None?"*

"Nary a one." Redfist settled in a massive wooden chair, a twin to the one I perched upon. All their furniture was on his scale, and though it appeared clean enough, I hesitated to lay even a knife upon the table. How could they not *bathe*? "There's oil and the *skauna*, instead."

Our dark-paneled, high-roofed wooden room was cozy enough, and Redfist had bargained hard and sharp for it. The innkeep, a black-browed giant with multicolored red-and-blue cloth bunched about his ample waist, had jabbed a thumb at me more than once, and Darik's glower had not dissuaded him one whit. Redfist had made little answer to the innkeep's questions, jests, or whatever they were, and I affected ignorant uncaring. Underfoot, the board floor was smooth enough, and the commonroom's grumble and bursts of sharp foreign laughter was welcome after the howling of the wind and the grinding of ice and rock.

There was even a *fire*, thank the Moon, though I

still shivered in my damp cloak. The warming-breath kept life in me, but even the discipline bred in G'mai-hallan might struggle with *this* freeze. "This does not sound sanitary."

"Neither does soaking in other people's piss like ye do doon south, K'na." He stretched his legs out, enjoying the space and freedom. I wondered if he would find a skirt like the other men wore here.

"Nobody pisses in a *bath*, Redfist." I stared at the flames, and the dull flush suffusing my cheeks might have been welcome in this cold place if he had not been so insulting. "That would be uncivilized."

His shrug was a mountain's shifting under heavy snow. Darik peered out the window. I will say, the North has fine glass. It is not the small diamond panes of the Rim's cities, or the tinted sheets of my homeland. Somehow, their glass is clear and beautiful, and they place in in square panes divided by iron and framed in wood. Much thinner than the Rim's, it nonetheless insulates marvelously well. Beyond its clear carapace, snow fell in steadily thickening clumps; we had brought weather with us from the Pass. It was a great comfort to be watching the white ice fall with its deceptively gentle kisses onto every surface than to be trudging in it, or camping in the chill stone cube of a waystation. Even better to be snug in a room of heavy lumber and too-big furnishings with a respectable fire.

Even if said fire did not warm me overmuch. I was well upon my way to hating this country, and that is never a good sign. I do not even hate Pesh outright, merely found it uncomfortable, and *that* land is as harsh as the Danhai plains in its own way.

"There's nae *skauna* for women, though." Redfist's cheeks had turned red as well. "Not in an inn."

I did not care where the women of his country

29

bathed, in river or streamlet, I merely wished to sluice the journey from my skin. "And not even a fall-water? How am I supposed to clean myself, Rainak Redfist? With sorcery?"

"Well, ye *are* elvish, and J'na was teaching you—"

"Redfist." I swallowed a hot flare of annoyance and pushed aside the urge to pull my heels up to rest upon the chair with me and hug my knees. "I dislike that word."

"Teaching?" Now he looked baffled, blue eyes wide and clear. He scratched at his furred neck with blunt fingertips, chasing an itch.

"Never mind." If he did not understand, at least he could not needle me about it in his rough way. My own scalp crawled, travel-dirt ground in among my braids. "I care little if this *skauna* does not take your countrywomen, but *I* will be clean."

"Then you'd best take both of us with ye to bathe, lass. Otherwise..."

What in the name of the gods is this? I pulled my damp cloak a little tighter. "Do you mean violence? Or rape? Or both?"

"Well, a girl in the *skauna*...a pretty girl, men will think..."

The incredible misapplication of the tradetongue for *pretty* was only the first problem with his hints and intimations. I had the strange sensation of the world shifting under me. "Men will think *what?*"

"Kaia..." He glanced at Darik, as if expecting help.

My *s'tarei* looked merely perplexed, sliding out of his cloak and hanging it upon a wooden rack near the fire. Maybe he found the fire enough to dispel the chill, but I was not so lucky. "Do you mean..." He paused, as if hesitant even to suggest such a thing, "that men of your country would offer my *adai* insult? While *bathing*?" He glanced at me, too, to see if I knew aught of this strangeness.

Redfist colored even more deeply, his cheeks rosy as fresh Shainakh bricks. "Some barstids might think to take advantage, aye."

"No wonder they all smell so foul," I muttered, sagging into the rudely constructed chair. One does not expect fine carvings or cuisine in a border-city inn, but still, the furniture here seemed barely sanded. A sword-sized splinter now seemed the least of my worries, however.

"Honest stench is nae bad thing." The giant shifted a little uncomfortably. I was, perhaps, keeping him from this oil and *skauna*, whatever it was.

I wanted to be clean and dry more than I wished to untangle the issue, though. "Tis not something I care to propagate, my barbarian friend."

It turned out the process is almost pleasant—a thick application of oil all over the body skimmed off with a bone tool, though the weedy (for a giant) young attendant blushed and would not wield it upon me. D'ri made a fair job of it, and I scraped him in turn while the young giant attended to Redfist and gawked. It was difficult to credit that the attendant may not have seen a naked woman before, and I wondered what he would make of the baths in Shai-tush or Antai's great marble temples to cleanliness. The bath-house is sacred. Even political rivals in Hain do not break the peace of fallwater-rinsing and long hot or tepid soaks.

The *skauna* was a small underground chamber, tiled on roof, walls, and floor, with heat rising through deep holes driven in the earth as well as fire-warmed rocks in a small depression in the floor. A ladleful of herbs and water is tossed over the rocks, and it is *almost* as pleasant as a bath, but not quite.

Redfist told me the traditional *skauna* ended with flinging oneself outside into a snowdrift, and my disbelieving laughter seemed to touch his pride. "Who would be foolish enough to do *that?*" I asked, between chuckles, and he glowered at me.

After the *skauna*-steam dissipates, one bakes in arid heat until wrung dry; snowmelt is often brought in by attendants for drinking, along with mead. Fortunately, none of Redfist's countrymen came to use tiny, hot room that night. Working my way into dry traveling clothes and consigning our wet cloth to the inn's staff was *particularly* pleasurable.

Ill-luck chose not to strike then, but at dinner.

A QUIET GATHERING

A METAL PLATTER bearing a great slab of meat is thumped upon a groaning table, surrounded by roasted, head-sized meatroots accompanied by pickled waxleaf, and crowded with great flowers of yeasted bread with a springy, chewy crumb. Strange implements are used to shovel this heavy fare into a Skaialan's face—handles with odd tines, tiny ladles on other handles, and small, sharp knives to carve bits of the meat free and spear the meatroots upon. The pickled waxleaf is strong and good, and the bread, but there was no green to be found. Great tankards of mead and a deep, bitter ale are brought, too. No wine, no *pirin* sauce, no fish—even dried—and no flatbread. No small bowls to hold your portion in, but wide wooden plates which are cleaned by sopping the bread in juices and detritus. I contented myself with part of a meatroot and the cabbage, and filled the rest of my belly's aching with the bread. A few swallows of the ale almost turned me green, so I turned to their mead and was pleasantly surprised. It is clear and fiery, full of spice, and summer-drowse can be tasted in its golden depths.

I was the only female guest in the commonroom.

Oh, there were Skaialan women with their light or ruddy hair piled atop their heads and wide brushing multicolored skirts of their strange weave, where each set of stripe-colors delineates a certain clan or family. But they served the food, refilled the tankards, and avoided the pinching, grasping hands of the men. Not even in Pesh had I seen such pawing and groping. The women wore loose linen shirts with a complicated truss about their middles, pushing great floury breasts high and showing a chasm like the Pass between.

And they are all so *pale*. If not for the different shades of beard and clothing, I might not be able to tell them apart. They are all uncooked dough, with mushroom noses and gleaming smiles. Some of them had gold on the tooth, an accoutrement I had not seen since Hain. There, it is a mark of high wealth, but in the Highlands it is merely a sign of rot. Later, I learned the pale gold Highlanders mine is prized more highly than the yellow, the latter only thought fit for dentistry. Shainakh's red gold is much in demand, though they perform an odd test to see if it is real—they rub it against their paler metal, to see if the two produce the proper smear upon each other's faces.

That evening, though, I luxuriated in eating my fill even if the fare was heavy. I suspected I would long for fish and flatbread soon, and even such humble greens as cressten or *baia*. I might even be reduced to eating the pungent needles of the trees on the mountainslopes, the ones who wear their deep prickling robes all year instead of stripping to dip into the tepid pool of winter. I watched the common-room, noting the sly glances in our direction. D'ri applied himself to the meat with a will, to replace flesh lost on the mountain slopes. The cold will melt everything extraneous off the bones before it strikes to kill, and the warming breath requires much fuel.

Uneasiness brushed my nape, cold fingers I could not blame on the wind outside. New arrivals slammed, swore, and yelled near the inn's front door. They have curious antechambers, perhaps to rob the weather of its sting, though they do not leave their shoes there as the Hain do. They track mud and snow in with abandon, especially at inns and taverns, and leave the traces of their passage in rushes or sweet-straw spread upon the floor. The stamping and shouting must be heard to be believed. Even the Shainakh irregulars at their most riotous could not produce anything near the sheer quantity of *noise*. Near the fire were two men playing curiously shaped lutes, and their music was interesting—at least, what little of it I could hear. Mud stippled their hairy calves and thick boots; they spread their legs wide and I received the impression that under the pleated material of their...skirts, I suppose?—they wore very little.

Redfist leaned back, patting his stomach, and loosed a prodigious belch. He took a long pull from his tankard—*proper* ale, he called it, and poured it down at an alarming rate—and beamed at me. "Feels good to be back!" He had to lean almost into my lap to be heard. "How do you like the roast? Wild *scruagh!*"

"'Tis very rich," I all-but-shouted back. "Is it always this *loud?*"

"Nae. This is *quiet* gathering, lass." His laugh was freighted with ale-smell, a healthy heat-haze I almost welcomed. Even in this crowded press, with the fire in the great hearth and the door to what had to be a kitchen swinging back and forth to belch heat, I could not warm myself. They say those from the

South have blood too thin to stand winter in the Highlands, and I can believe it. The warming-breath kept me from freezing outright, but only just.

Thank the gods I had not braved this place before Janaire's teachings and the *taih'adai*, or I would have turned to an ice-statue in the Pass itself and never seen what lay beyond.

Yet more Skaialan stamped into the common-room, two man-mountains with their cloaks streaming snowmelt. A roar of laughter went up, and my swordhand itched. I saw the smaller of the two newcomers glance once across the room, and the flat murderous sheen upon his eyes sent a bolt of *wrong* through me. Our gazes met, and the shorter man-mountain saw Rainak Redfist. A flash of recognition and a crafty little gleam on those pale, ratlike eyes were all the warning I needed.

I laid my eating-picks down, carefully, and D'ri tensed on my other side. Redfist, his eyes blissfully closed, tilted a fresh tankard brought by a harried, pale-haired wench. I disliked the idea of heaving a sotted barbarian up the stairs to our room, but the thought was very far away. My hand blurred for my *dotani*-hilt, and I shoved my chair back, its legs scrape-screaming through a rime of mud dried to a paste from its last inhabitant. My left boot landed on the table and I *flew*, barely clearing the roast, my *dotani* blurring solid silver.

The Skaialan carry axe, flail, or sword. Said swords are much longer and heavier than even Danhai pigstickers, straight and with functional guards. Those blades can carve a man's face off, or even cut a child in half; I have seen as much. They are terrible weapons, but only if they catch you. Some northern giants are quicker than one would suspect; I had seen Redfist's deceptive speed and curious grace as he wielded his axe. A flail-wielder might have given me pause, if he could have untangled his weapon from the fat-dripping lightrack depending from the ceiling on an ornate iron chain. As it was, the first battle-eyed barbarian managed to unlimber his blade and raise it while I was gaining speed. His cloak, bunched over his breast and secured with a heavy, curiously-shaped pin-and-lutecurve, would blunt the force of any strike I could deliver. A collective gasp, chairs moving, the taller one reaching for what had to be a knifehilt, and I would down him too if I could just move quickly enough.

My *dotani* dipped, biting, and I had judged the strike aright. Even the largest of barbarians cannot absorb a sword to the throat.

A bright spray of blood, chaos erupting around me, and the taller one yelled something in Skaialan. Redfist was on his feet, drawing breath to bellow, his axe hefted and the blade glinting dully. Not the best weapon for close combat; neither is a *dotani* but a G'-maihallan sword looks a paring-knife when compared to their gigantic blades. My opponent spasmed, throwing out a meaty arm, and the sudden change in his weight threatened to drag me with him. I pitched sideways, my boot sinking just above his hip as I *wrenched*, and the grating of my blade on cervical vertebrae jolted up my arm.

A glitter streaked past; I almost saw the knifeblade cleaving air. It clanged dully—had it hit Redfist?—and battlerage made every movement other than mine slow and clumsy. My longest knife, jerked free of its sheath, slapped against my forearm, and there was precious little chance I would be able to pull my *dotani* free.

In a battle, though, one uses anything to hand. My grip changed as the smaller barbarian began to fall, his arms turned to headless snakes as blood and breath both left him. My *dotani* blade tore free, and I slid on my knees across the mud-spattered floor, my trews might not survive the splinters but I did not *care*, sweet wine-red jolts of pain up my knees. I was no longer truly young, but the experience of many battles may stand for youth's speed and flexibility— once survived, that is.

The taller one had his sword unlimbered and lifted—the knife *had* been meant for Redfist—and his mouth was a wide wet O as he yelled. I heard the trailing cry.

"*Ferulaaaaaaine!*"

It meant nothing, because I was where I needed to be now, almost *under* him. My left fist hit my right shoulder as I prepared the knife-strike, my entire body tensing as I stabbed upward, under his pleated, multicolored skirt. My *dotani* rang as it I next pitched myself the *other* way, a weak slash darting for his belly.

My knife sank into his thigh, angled precisely for the artery; I *twisted* and wrenched as much as I could before the hilt ripped from my hand. His bellowing turned into something very like a harpy's scream. I didn't have much strength behind my *dotani* strike, but even a weak slash was enough to force him backward. His leg buckled; I scrabbled back on shoulders and heels, *move or be crushed, Kaia*, and a dark thunderbolt was Darik, leaping to kick. All the force he could gather thudded with his boot in the taller man's gut, and my *s'tarei* dropped immediately as it transferred. His boots thudded on either side of my hips, and I had to take care I did not spit him with my own blade. I kept scrabbling back, and Redfist's roar —better late than never—was accompanied by a great crashing.

I gained my feet with a muscle-tearing lunge, whirling and bringing my *dotani* up. The throat-slit giant had taken two faltering steps and toppled sideways, landing upon the edge of another table crowded with empty tankards and surrounded by three sourfaced Skaialan who had been busily trying to drink themselves into the afterworld. As it was, they barely noticed, merely shouting what I took to be abuse at the sudden bump. One shoved the falling body aside to land on the floor instead of disturbing their drinking further. Another, a black-bearded giant with small bones—they looked very much like tiny harpy beaks—tied into his beard and hair, held aloft his grimy tankard and pounded his other fist on the sadly abused table, calling for another drink.

Not much disturbs a Skaialan who has seriously set himself to ale-deaden his wits.

There was little danger from that quarter, so I turned back. D'ri regarded the taller giant on the floor, the lake of blood underneath rapidly growing. Bleeding from the thigh's great Shelt-channel is difficult to stem; I had seen battlefield healers loosen bandages to let a sellsword die quickly instead of seeking to stanch it. There are very few methods for treating such a wound. Perhaps an *adai* skilled in flesh-mending could do so, but I was not.

Nor did I wish to be, at that moment.

The innkeep, a proud-bellied and soft-shouldered mass in a much-bleached apron, wrung his hands at the far end of the commonroom, lowing like a distressed calf. Redfist shoved a spectator who had pushed too close to the brawl, and unless I missed my guess, there were several rounds of *betting* going on, small counters passed from hand to hand and a number of sausage-fat fingers pointed in my direction. I whipped my dotani to clean it, yanking a bit of rag from my clothpurse to rub the shining blade, checking for chips along the edge.

Sometimes, bone will bite back.

There did not appear to be any more danger. Redfist engaged in a volley of their strange language with the innkeep, and I met D'ri's gaze as he glanced over his shoulder to see if I was well. I nodded, slightly, and he straightened, returning his attention to the rapidly dying meat on the floor.

The giant's lips, strangely chalky from the bloodloss, shaped the syllables again. "*Ferulaaaine,*" he whispered, and sagged against the floor. His bowels released, a sharp stink that sent an excited murmur through the commonroom.

Oddly enough, I felt more at home. A tavern brawl is much the same in every corner of the world. Except G'maihallan, where such things are all but unknown. No *s'tarei* will risk the life of an *adai* in such a fashion, even one not their own.

I placed the word. *Ferulaine.* The clan-name of Dunkast, who had sent pale Northern gold to Antai.

Redfist's great enemy.

How very interesting.

BATTLEFIELD MERCY

"Tıs a fine mess." Redfist folded his arms over his barrel chest, glowering into our sullen-embered fireplace. "The innkeep threatened to throw us into the snows, Kaia."

"So I should have let them kill you?" I frowned at my largest knife. The tip was blunted, so I drew it along the whetstone at the proper angle. Our room was a small ship in a tempest, to judge by the noise from downstairs. Would sleep even be possible in such a setting? "I shall remember that, friend Redfist, next time there is fighting to be done."

He did not rise to the bait. "They were *Ferulaine.*"

I quelled a needle-prick of irritation that he would address me as if I lacked wit or the will to use it. At least I did not have blood in my hair, though my scalp crawled. I longed for a proper bath. "So I gathered. Somehow related to this Dunkast, perchance?"

"His is a bastard's clan, so there is nae blood, but it doesnae make them less kin. No doubt there would be a rich prize if they managed to take my head." Redfist's frown was thunderous as he crouched to feed the fire with chunks of the North's fine black fire-rock, and his club of red hair, newly wrapped,

41

could have been used as a weapon too. "Word will spread I've returned, and sooner than I thought. Ye could have looked away, Kaia."

"He was already drawing a knife." Another scraping against the whetstone matched the rasp against my nerves, and I tried not to feel ill-tempered. The bodies had been heaved outside; the large, feral *torkascruagh* roaming the streets of Karnaugh would take care of *them* in short order. D'ri lifted one of my braids, tucking it back into the complex arrangement; he even retied the bit of coarse string keeping it confined. He had grown more facile at such things, of late, and it was strange to feel another's fingers in my hair. Sometimes Kesa at the Swallows Moon had braided it Clau-fashion, in loops over the ears and a rope down the back, but I prefer the crowning styles of my homeland. They cannot be grasped by an enemy, and they cushion a helm wonderfully, though I rarely wear more than an archer's light leather cap.

I need to see what I am killing.

Redfist sighed. "There is only your word for that."

My hands halted their familiar motion. Darik's touch left my hair, and before I could open my mouth, he saved me the trouble.

"Do you accuse my *adai* of an untruth, barbarian?" Cold and formal even in tradetongue, and if D'ri did not add a curse or two in G'mai, it was perhaps only because politeness is bred into our kind, and palace training would have doubled the dose. It was an oblique warmth, that he would take issue with such a thing.

"Of course not." Redfist's brow was ferociously knotted, and the barbarian wasn't even looking at me. He scrubbed his palms against his trouser-knee, ridding them of soot. "I am thinking of how it looked to everyone else in the commonroom."

"Ah." I stared at the knifeblade. "You thought you had time to gather something in secret, friend Redfist, but the game was already given away. Ninefingers no doubt sent word he had found you."

"Ye cannot know that."

You ignorant piece of lard. I drew the stone up the knifeblade, a ringing scrape. Outside, a wailing white wind had closed over Karnaugh's red roofs. "Did you not notice their cloaks? They had been tramping for hours. Why do that, *here?* And both of them reeked of drink, but not enough to make them sloppy. *And* they recognized you. Why would they, if they had not been warned? *He is this tall, and this redhaired, and he will be wearing Southron cloth.*" The knifetip was repairable, but not while I was in this mood. I would no doubt cut myself, and deserve it richly for disrespecting a blade. "Mother's *tits*, Redfist, do you think I would simply kill them for their looks?"

"I noticed their cloaks. And aye, I knew neither of their faces." Redfist stamped to a chair and flung himself into it, slumping. With his brawny arms crossed and his chin dipped, he looked like one of the puppets the R'jiin use to make children laugh. Their tales of the far North are full of shadows and strange noises, and I could well believe one or two of them might have traveled in these lands to bring such things back. "I do not blame ye, Kaia. Ye're more like a *wal'kir* than ever, and I a puling child to be making such noises. Forgive me."

An honest apology eases tension as few other things can, and I nodded. "Forgiven. What is this *vollkyir?*"

"Shield-maids." The tip of his nose pinkened.

"Shieldwives?" I could not quite believe my ears. "That is hardly complimentary."

"Maybe nae in your tongue, but in mine tis a high honor. A *wal'kir* holds a sword, and grants men mercy on the battlefield."

"A healer?" Now *that* was interesting. I had never been called such before. I eyed the highly-patterned woven rug before the fireplace, its rough nap no doubt shaken free of mud between each set of guests. If they did not wash their bodies, did they wash their linens, at least?

"No, lass." He stretched his long legs, and at least here in his country there was space for such a maneuver. "Mercy with a blade, when the body is too shattered for mending."

"Ah." Tis a job no sellsword likes. *To draw the Reaper's straw*, the Shainakh call it, and those who perform it are given double rations of hanta to ease the task, and the conscience afterward.

"There are stories of them riding with the gods of battle, as the blackwing birds do. Sometimes, when a lass dies in childbirth, she becomes one." Redfist's cheeks had gone pale. "We see them in battle, when Kroth is unusually interested in the outcome or the blood."

"I see. The Danhai had something similar." When the women of the grass seas mourned—usually after losing their children to invaders' swords—they sometimes cut their hair, paint their faces with ash, and become terrors of night and wind, able to hide behind a single blade of grass and put an arrow through a faraway coney's eye. You could not take an ash-ghost prisoner. I had seen one bite through her own tongue and bleed to death while clapped in chains.

I did not blame her. Danhai women in Shainakh army camps are few, and they do not survive long.

The longer I was on the plains, the more I blamed the fat, greedy Shainakh Emperor Azkillian for all the death, despair, and hideousness than any tribefolk *or* my fellow sellswords. I had joined the irregulars to escape other troubles, and wondered ever since if I had been too honorable for my own good. Or—and this was the troublesome part—not as honorable as I thought I was.

As I wished to be, as I had *decided* to be when I left G'maihallan so many seasons ago.

"Do they now." Redfist loosened enough to stroke at his beard, thoughtfully. He was removing the beads from its flow, one or two at a time. Perhaps he was shedding the South now that he was home. Had he considered the Rim as barbaric as I considered this hellish place?

Darik settled on a tall three-legged stool near my chair and began checking his own knives, perhaps merely to keep his hands busy. His silence was not uncomfortable, but it *was* watchful, and I had known him long enough, finally, to tell the difference.

"What is your next move?" I did not sound very curious, only weary. Gods knew I felt the distance from civilization like a heavy weight in all my joints, and the cold nipped at my ear-tips, fingers, and toes.

Redfist considered me, but his gaze had turned inward, traveling upon memory-roads. "Well now, perhaps resting a bit would be wise. But I never was *that*. Kalburn is our goal. Further north, and traders will be traveling between now and deepwinter. Best place to wait out the treecrack."

Treecrack? That does not sound amusing at all. "Defensible?" I set knife and sheathe on the table, and longed for chai. For *pirin* sauce, and some pungent *baia*. Not to mention flatbread, and…

Gods, I was growing querulous in my age. Soon I would be an old sellsword complaining of her bowels and shirking what duties I could.

"Not so much." Redfist's smile, for once, was not cheerful at all. More like a grimace, but that managed to hearten me a little. "But once I reach the Standing Stones, I may call the clans."

That sounds promising. "Very well, then." I scrubbed at my face with both hands though no bloodmist had landed upon my cheeks. At least the rest of our troupe was safe in Antai, perhaps looking through the same windows I had thought to watch the rains from. "I hope we may sleep before we leave."

A TRICKSOME BUSINESS

THAT NIGHT the white wind descended from the North, striking the mountains behind Karnaugh with furious screams, but the Skaialan are a hardy people. In the gray chill of morning we ventured forth to find passage.

There were caravans leaving—Antai is not the only part of the world where profit strikes the cadence all dance to—and one was happy enough to hire Redfist as an outrider, that sellsword insurance against bandits. D'ri and I, as foreigners, were added by dint of Redfist arguing vociferously that his companions were better protection than a few Skaialan giants. Salden the caravan master, in tradetongue liberally spattered with Skaialan obscenities, called me a cheap courtesan one too many times, and I bloodied his nose despite having to leap to reach it. He went down hard, and I added a few more blows for good measure until Redfist lifted me off by my belt and shoulder. The caravan-master's fellows, mostly shorter than Redfist but not by much, roared with laughter, and Darik took his hand away from his *dotanii* hilts before they glimpsed his readiness.

That settled matters, and we were added to the

caravan as well. Our ponies were left in the care of a livery, and I made certain they understood the beasts were to be treated well until I returned.

I did not think it prudent to admit, even to myself, that I might not.

So, we set out for Kalburn, and the Standing Stones.

Skaialan caravans are made of slow-moving, high-roofed waggons, pulled not by oxen but by *torkascruagh*, their tusk-teeth painted with ochre like the Hain dye their plow-oxen's horns. The conveyances creak and roll along roads cunningly laid to be swept clean by wind or shielded from the worst drifts; sometimes curious structures are erected to channel the force of the weather and keep a passage clear. Strung out upon a road, a caravan creaks and rattles, and the outriders either crowd close or spread into the snow atop their stamping, snorting, shaggy steeds. A *torkascruagh's* saddle is a high-cantled affair, meant to keep one in its grasp even during a full gallop. The creatures are capable of short bursts of amazing speed, but their real usefulness lies in their patient, indefatigable plodding. They can walk all day, and all night, as long as they are given enough forage. Their stomachs are not fussy, either—they can, and will, eat almost anything. There are many proverbs in the North about their capacity to consume, and after any battle the creatures eat well of the fallen.

I have witnessed as much with my own eyes.

The first night, D'ri and I bedded down in one of the shell-like tents, upon a fragrant bed of stacked *poila* branches with their heavy green needles. One of the waggon-hands blundered against the side of the tent, mead-soaked and mumbling something that did not sound at all polite, and Darik nearly killed him. I heard an argument, and peered out to see Redfist shaking the big, blond, malodorous man by the front of his fur-lined cloak-coat, snarling in their language. It took a few moments before I understood.

There were no women with the caravan. Like the Pesh, they keep daughters, wives, and mothers home-fast; if a woman travels the North she must have a protector or be extremely handy with a blade *and* keep watch even while sleeping. It is not so different from some places on the Rim, but there are not even female sellswords in Redfist's homeland.

They have songs about warrior women, of course, and songs about women stabbing a faithless lover or protecting their homes with their carving-knives. There is even a brand of witchery many Skaialan women practice, and one adept at it may eventually, after her childbearing years are done, become what they call a *morigwyn*, a wise-woman, something very close to a Yada'Adais. The black-winged mother of their god Kroth looks upon *morigwyni* with favor and strikes those who insult them with boils, but until they are rolled in black fabric and old age women do not travel alone.

We made friends with our *torkascruagh*, D'ri and I. When you are riding a wall of shaggy meat with a mouth that can take your head off, it is very good to be friendly. He named his beast *Atlara*, a word that could have meant *one-tooth* or *moving sharpness*, used to describe the shape of certain mountains in G'mai-hallan. It had two tusks, but the joke had driven me to a fit of coughing mirth the first night he used it, so it became a name. My own I called *Guilnor*, a Ska-ialan child-word for a midden-heap. The creatures slept between our shell-tent and a waggon with its "skirts" dropped; they alerted us once or twice to trouble with their restlessness. The other outriders—

three, not including Redfist—had perhaps thought to mock the foreigners by giving us the most ill-tempered of the brood, but after making my *s'tarei's* acquaintance, they became docile as our left-behind ponies.

I did not dream—there was no time for it. The waggons may become bogged, there is game to be hunted even in the white wastes, and there are wild *torkascruagh* to be reckoned with as well, ever alert for something to eat. A large one in a fury can crack a waggon in half.

Then, there were the bandits.

There is a god with a grasp as tight as profit, and its name is desperation. Listening at the nightly fire, as a cauldron of thick, pungent stew bubbled over a flame I had more than once coaxed into being without a sparkstone—the first time I performed *that* trick they all fell silent, like large children, and Redfist murmured that they had best be careful of my temper—I heard a familiar tale as my grasp of their language firmed, of men driven into the wilderness by heavy debt or vengeance, roaming without clan or chieftain. The harvest had been fine this year, especially in the black-soiled valleys, but the man in the North had taken a great deal as toll and tax.

I thought your kind had no kings, I said once, to Redfist, who looked pained.

Seems we've one now in all but name, he growled in response, and said no more.

Consolidating power is always a tricksome business. The Shainakh, conquerors grown fat and custom-bound, took large swathes of the Danhai grassland almost at will, but they could not *hold* it. The freetowns along the Rim squabbled too much to be a proper empire, but if one were threatened by larger neighbors they stood together, knowing full well the risks otherwise. Pesh raided the hills for fresh slaves; their neighbors the Bha-gra of the deserts could not seem to unite though they had once been a horde under a veiled woman claimed to be half goddess. Tar-Amyarat had married into their conquerors, and Clau's voracious island gods had absorbed theirs too. Even the Pensari had fallen, but in their day, when they came cold and raving from the Breaking Pillars, those who knelt survived. To build an empire one must have cunning and foresight as well as power, not to mention deep coffers and the means to instill fear.

It seemed this Dunkast had deep coffers, for he now owned many of the mines that produced their pale gold. And, given by the way they whispered *the man in the North* instead of his name, he had fear at his command. Cunning and foresight?

Well, time and again Redfist would ask of one clan or another, one name or another, sometimes casually, sometimes wonderingly. The answer was always the same: either said man had bowed to the Ferulaine...or an accident had occurred. The tolls paid to the Crae had been merely custom, and traditionally, any who demanded much else were swiftly replaced.

But now, when the man in the North asked, a Skaialan was forced to give or to die. Or to become a bandit.

A long tale, yes, but must be told in order to understand the almost-daily attacks, sometimes even coming from the deep forest after the nooning. If not for the clumsiness of their bows, we might all have bled into the snows. Daylight attacks began with a deep-throated yell, and whatever ragged band of hungry ghost-giants had spotted us wending our slow creaking way along the slice of road they laid claim to would burst from the trees. The *torkascruagh* would begin to bellow, and it would be time to earn our coin *and* our meals.

The waggon-hands were handy enough with staves, but their concern was the goods piled in their wooden boats upon the snowy sea. During day attacks, the four Skaialan outriders circled, and I went wherever I was needed, Darik at my back like a shadow, our *torkascruagh* bellowing and tossing their heads as the attackers, on foot, did their best.

Very few of the bandits rode in order to trouble us. The wild *torkascruagh* are not very amenable, and the beasts needed more forage than threadbare, starving ruffians can procure. More often, attackers crept in with darkness, sometimes under the cover of white winds, and it was night-fighting in the deadly cold. Except for the forest drawing close, it was like the plains again, nerves pulled taut at each moment, even while you pissed. Wells of darkness between massive trees holding their soft green fragrant needles can hide all manner of danger. The Skaialan greased their faces and calves with fat to keep the grayrot-freeze from eating their flesh. My ear-tips were perpetually numb, my stomach always unhappy, the warming breath second nature by now, and whatever warmth I could gather huddled against Darik in our shell-tent was not enough for more than fitful rest.

When it warmed slightly the snow came and became a cold wet weight against every struggling movement. When the sky cleared, the temperature plunged, and a gobbet of spit could crackle into ice mid-air. If not for the *taih-adai* and Janaire's careful tutelage, I might have frozen to death more than once; if not for D'ri at my back, I might have had to kill more than one of the outriders *and* no few of the waggon-hands as well.

Just when it seemed we had slid into an ice-bound hellish afterlife, doomed to an eternity of hauling ourselves forward by painful increments, we eased down three days' worth of a long incline and arrived at a valley that, while still cold as one of the Hain ideas of hell, was *not* under multiple armlengths of killing white. The sky was still iron-colored, but there was long sere winter grass and tough, spiny green bushes loaded with tart, pungent, small black fruit. The *torkascruagh* stopped wheezing and pricked their tasseled ears, smelling the reek of settlement.

One thing about riding the beasts: I could draw one leg up, hooking it around the cantle, and ride for a long while without splitting like a Rijiin acrobat. The stretching was no doubt good for me—every knife-fighter needs flexibility in the hips—but not for twelve candlemarks at a time.

Far away, at the end of a gently curving mud-track, smoke rose from a walled town with a high-stretched cube of stone rising in its center. I eyed the terrain—broken mountains lay shattered to the west, curving slightly around the north. The valley was large, more properly a plain cupped among the earth-gods' smashed plates. Steam vented from relatively small fissures—heat from below the earth, I realized, the breath and boiling blood of the great wingwyrm coiled at the world's core. The city was old enough to have sprawled outside its original, eminently defensible walls in every direction, giants laying claim to space the same way any other folk do.

Since we approached Kalburn from the south, we did not see the Standing Stones. They tell tales of their highgod Kroth striking the valley with his hammer, calling forth the fires at the heart of the world in his battle with a wolf made of darkness. The Stones, milky columns alight with blushing veins, stand in an irregular circle a half-candlemark ride from Kalburn's northern edge, and tis said that to wind a horn in their center will make it heard throughout the Highlands. That is, if you can *reach* the center of their stony floor, and if you do not wish to strike the altar at its center with the great hammer—but that came later.

We reached the fringes of the settlement before nightfall, and took our pay from the relieved Salden, who would realize a hefty profit from all goods arriving intact.

Salden *also* tried to pay me half the promised price, after he had already paid Redfist and D'ri. He relented when I laid hand to hilt, and the greasy surprise on his face when Darik did not move to restrain me filled me with weary revulsion.

"Outlander whore," he snarled, through the ice drip-melting from his beard.

"May you be hanged," I retorted, in passable Skaialan. It is a great insult to them, to die suspended rather than on the battlefield. I do not know which of us was more maligned, but I had my coil of silver Northern tradewire and left him in the long chilly shed of a counting-house where his goods would be unloaded and weighed before his clients came to take possession of them. He would find more cargo and leave with his waggon-hands and his three Skaialan outriders, and I wished him joy of his further journeys.

Joy, and many a bandit raid.

A KING NOW

REDFIST CHOSE the largest inn outside the walls of Kalburn's Old City, a throbbing stone-and-timber heap full of outriders, caravaneers, and other flotsam with enough coin to shelter in some comfort. His impatience might have dragged us directly into trouble the next morning, had not a curious bit of news filtered into the commonroom.

"Every gate to Kalburn is watched. And all the roads going south. North, not so much." Redfist frowned, his chin almost touching his chest, making his teeth shy white ponies behind ruddy bushes. He still wore his southron clothing, though he had added a great brown furred cloak to keep the wind away. "They search each caravan as it leaves."

"Who does?" I poked at the bowl of thick, toothrot-sweet gruel that mimicked breakfast here. It was passable, if one crumbled some pungent white cheese into its gray depths, but it could not be eaten with picks. I was loath to use my fingers, and the implements they used were a extremely awkward. The small flattened ladles—spoons—used to shovel the glop into their faces were nowhere near as cleanly as picks. You had to put the whole *bowl* in your mouth, heaped high with the thick bits of porridge, and suck it clean.

That was disconcerting enough, and the glances and whispers when I appeared were too. I had not felt so ill-placed since my first trip across the Lan'ai. At least with my braids hiding my ear-tips I could pass for a mixture of some sort along the Rim, but here among the pale giants, copper skin and slightness of stature made me an oddity. D'ri they also watched, but not nearly as closely.

"Ferulaine toll-takers." It might as well have been an obscenity, the way his face turned sour. He added a few terms in Skaialan I was pleased to be able to decipher. "Tis worse than I thought."

"How?" I had largely mastered the accents in his language, and he often looked gratified for a moment or so at my careful study before repeating stray terms with the correct pronunciation. Now that I heard his tongue spoken all around me, much of how he weighted his tradetongue was explained.

He now salted his tradetongue with as much Skaialan as it could bear, too. "None of the Crae ha' ever set *tolls* before. Tis not the Highland way. I was in the marketplace before sunup, and the news is whispered instead of shouted as it should be. Tis as if they think he can hear them."

"Is he here?" I managed my own Skaialan creditably well. It would take a while, but their tongue is direct and *much* less complex than G'mai. It was a good thing I had learned my Shainakh and my tradetongue so assiduously. Each language one manages to store in one's head is an insurance, and makes the learning of others easier.

"No. At Ferulaine. He's claimed a space far North and built a keep there, too." Redfist's blue eyes glittered. He had lost the air of grudging delicacy he practiced with smaller southron tables, chairs, and other implements, and was no doubt relieved to have done so. "Been gone too long, I have. Tis as if he is daring me to come for him."

I glanced at the stairs at the far end of the commonroom—Darik's familiar tread upon them was a relief. He looked just as cold as I felt, the tips of his ears reddened and his bladed nose pink, and when he settled beside me I did not mind him moving close enough for our hips to touch. It was dangerous not to leave a space to bring a blade free, but worth it to feel his warmth. He thanked the inngirl who brought him a bowl of the gruel with quiet courtesy in tradetongue, and *her* cheeks flushed. Perhaps it was because of his strangeness, though I should think they would call him handsome enough in any land.

"What manner of keep?" I traced an outline upon the tabletop, the shape of the city I had seen so far. Karnaugh is a fastness merely from the south, its wall placed both to discourage banditry and break some of the force of the Pass's howling. Kalburn was otherwise—the ancient wall held mayhap a quarter of the city, the rest spreading along road-arteries according to the dictates of trade. The Keep here was well-built of a single block of stone thrust from the earth by some titanic convulsion, but relatively small for all it dominates that part of the valley-plain.

"A fine one, they say, and there are stories of the blocks quarried for it dancing into place of their own accord." Redfist glowered afresh at his breakfast, a pastry pocket of something smelling suspiciously like heavily spiced *torkascruagh* innards.

D'ri tested porridge with his own spoon and glanced at me. "Using Power to shift stones is not uncommon in our land."

"Well, this is the North, boyo." Redfist took another large bite, barely chewing before washing the mess down with a draft of weak, chunky-thick morning-ale. "And tis damn unnatural for a bastard clan to build a keep to surpass all others in a single season."

I considered this new tale. "He did this within a summer? A *single* summer?"

"Aye." Redfist's glower deepened, and he made a sweeping motion, catching the eye of the slow-moving inngirl, for another mug of the heavy, yeasty almost-bread they drank with their morning meal. "Five years I've been gone, and Corran did not tell me the half of it."

"He was not paid to," I pointed out. But softly, for I did not wish to argue or distract. "So, he has a keep in the north and is collecting tolls. Kingly business indeed."

"A curst business, instead." He shouted something at the inngirl, who replied in kind. "There's none of yer kafi here, Kaia, nor your chai, but I've something better."

"Tis hard to see how chai could be improved upon. And your country-fellows, do you think they are pleased to have a ruler?" I dragged my spoon through porridge, a channel dug in silty mud. "Try it with the cheese," I told D'ri, whose look suggested I had perhaps lost my senses, but he reached for the bowl full of crumbling, pungent curds.

I did not see many cattle, but the weather was such I did not wonder much at it. And if they milked the *torkascruagh*, I did not wish to know.

"I know what they are." Redfist paused as the inngirl, hissing an imprecation, brought three high, wide mugs to the table. He laughed and reached to slap at her hindquarters, but she was light on her feet for such a tall ample-hipped woman. I swallowed a disgusted sigh. Twas a good thing *I* was not an inngirl, I would have lopped a few hands from their bearers by now.

And—useless to deny it—the Redfist within Ska-ialan borders was not the same man as the Redfist outside. I had called him barbarian all this time, and now that we were in his homeland, he seemed determined to be one. I found myself longing for civilization, for a long hot bath, and for less bloodshed and better weather. Not for the first time, I might add.

Definitely not for the last, either.

"And what is that?" D'ri took a mouthful of his porridge, and a curious look crossed his face. I banished a small smile, knowing from the way his eyebrows rose that he found the taste strange but not unpleasant.

Redfist did not smile. He did not even manage to look happy at the new addition to our breakfast. "Afraid."

"Of whatever witchery this Dunka-est found?" My pronunciation had grown better. At least, I hoped it had.

"That, and more." He pushed his ale-mug aside, which was a relief. Or table was much quieter than many others, and tucked into a corner besides. "I like not the sound of this, lass, and it seems entering Kalburn will be difficult. We've come this far, but—"

"Entering a city is never *too* difficult, friend Redfist." I blew across the top of the bubbling white liquid in the mug, took a cautious sniff. It smelled… spicy, and oddly sweet. "What on earth is this?"

"*Sofin,*" he said, and repeated it until I found the right pronunciation. Then he sighed, and took a large pull of his own mug, despite the heat of the beverage. "And how do you crack a walled city in winter, with guards and toll-takers at every gate, hm? We only escaped search because Salden is known to pay hand-somely to avoid such things."

"You chose well." *I might have liked him more, had I known as much.* "And aye, walls are a problem. But a small one for a thief. A much larger one is the rumor of your presence drawing more blackened blades. I cannot kill *every* assassin in the world at once."

Whatever reply he might have made was lost in a swelling tide of whispers and low whistles as someone stamped in the entryway, a quick light ha-bitual double-tap to rid boots of snow. The heavy strips of cloth hung at the inner end of the entry-chamber swayed gently as cold from outside moved the air in unsteady eddies. A fair-haired Skaialan woman appeared between the felted strips, sweeping them aside with one pale hand, and Redfist stiffened as if struck.

The woman had creamy cheeks and a proud nose, wide gray eyes and sun-yellow hair; she wore a volu-minous blue cloak trimmed with fine fur. A fillet of silver kept that hair back; two thick fair braids dipped over her shoulders and swayed gently as she moved. She looked nervous; her ear-drops—pretty, but not worth stealing—had glittering blue stones and swung as she scanned the commonroom.

Redfist gained his feet with a lunge. I had rarely seen him move so quickly even in battle, and he threaded between the sparsely inhabited common-room tables rather like an iron splinter following a lodestone. D'ri's left hand rested on a knifehilt, and I was about to rise when the woman's face went through several changes, settling into a paradoxical mixture of recognition and wondering surprise.

"Rainak—" Her lips shaped his name. She looked altogether too warm for the weather's chill fingers, and too clean for the mud coating even the cobbled ways of this place.

Our barbarian bore down upon her, caught her by the shoulders, and kissed her hard enough to bend her backward.

EMRATH

"I THOUGHT IT A LIE, but I had to see." Her tradetongue was stilted, but fair enough. She stood near the fireplace in our room, first glancing at Red-fist and then, curiously, at D'ri, who had brought his bowl—and the strange spoon—with him; she jabbed a fingertip at my *s'tarei*. "You, *susnach*, you great walloping idiot. Why have you brought Rainak here?"

D'ri glanced at me. I contented myself with locking the door and leaning against it with my ears pricked for any undue noises in the hallway, cupping my heavy earthenware mug of the queer white sofin. She had not given me much scrutiny, but I did otherwise.

This woman did not wear the low white blouse and high-laced vest of the inngirls, baring her flour-pale breasts as they did. Instead, her dress was high-necked, made of fine soft blue cloth, and the multi-colored skirts were divided unless I missed my guess, a form of wrapped and pleated material mimicking the mens' costume. Her cloak had sleeves, and its lining was plush-thick and delicate at the same time, some kind of spotted fur. Redfist's hands had left grease-marks upon her shoulders, but she did not seem to mind. Felted underboots and curious over-shoes tied with crosslaces peeped out from under her skirts, and both feet and skirts were too clean. Wherever she housed, she had not walked here.

Interesting. I took a sip, and found the beverage burned all the way down, a pleasant fire reminding one of sweetened chai. So far, the drink was the best thing in this icy hell.

The woman all but stamped her large shapely feet, still addressing Darik. "Why did you bring him back, *susnach*? Answer me!"

My *s'tarei* inclined his head slightly, glanced at me. I shook my head a fraction—let her see what rudeness gained her, this Northern woman—and he instead settled at the small table near the fireplace with his bowl. He could not ignore her more pointedly.

"I brought myself, Emrath." Redfist cleared his throat. "And do nae be ill-mannered to my friends. Kaai and Durrak here have saved my life many a time."

She rounded upon him, then, her skirts swaying with the motion. "Then what are you about, *here*? Kroth smite you, Rainak Redfist, for—"

"And what are *you* about, in such fine thread?" Redfist dropped Skaialan words into tradetongue instead of using them exclusively; either he was simply in the habit of doing it by now or he wanted to make certain I understood. The fire crackled uneasily, built back up from its morning embers. "The Lady of Kalburn never used to wear such things."

"Ye came to discuss my dresses?" She held up her left hand, pale Highland gold glittering at the base of her second and third fingers. The rings were joined, and angular runes chased their surfaces. "Or my shiny bits?"

Redfists's hands knotted, released as he went even

paler than his wont. Blue eyes glittered dangerously. "Who?" The single word, burred out in Skaialan, held a note I had never heard from my barbarian friend before.

The woman's hand dropped. "How did ye think ye were released? *He* wanted Kalburn, and I wanted you alive."

Redfist stared at her, pupils shrinking to pinpoints, and I wondered if he was going to strangle this new arrival. The blood now rising to his cheeks would not recede easily, if at all; from paleness to ruddy fury he had climbed in an instant.

The Northern woman continued, her tone rising to match. "I held him off as long as I could. With you gone, there was no reason to...and now here you are, and all of it for *nothing*." She looked ready to meet him blow for blow, too. It did not seem quite *right* that she had entered alone, given her fellow Highlanders and their habits. Most likely, her guards waited outside.

Hers, or...ah. There was only one possibility that made sense. "She married this Ferulaine." I folded my arms. "No doubt one or two loyal to him are outside." *Or in the commonroom by now.* My boots weren't even *dry* yet, and I might have to kill in a tavern brawl once more.

I did not think Redfist would be grateful.

The silence that fell was broken only by the soft sound of D'ri finishing his gruel. I took another sip of the *sofin*, deciding I might more than like it, and I held the Skaialan woman's gray gaze.

"What is *that*?" She did not point at me, but I suspected it was close. "A wee dark elvish bint in trousers?"

Mother's tits, *I hate that word.* I addressed my barbarian friend. "Do we kill her, or not?"

"We'll not be killing her, K'ai." Redfist sounded as if the air had been forced from him by a heavy blow. His use-name for me was often shortened to a single syllable, now that we were in his country and his accent had thickened. "At least not today. So, Needleslay's daughter, lady of Kalburn, did ye bring men with ye to restrain me as a criminal?"

"You are an *idiot*," she hissed, and I took a long hot draft of sofin. There did not seem to be any alcohol in it, which was probably for the best. D'ri set his bowl down, quickly and neatly, his nose wrinkling a little at the gruel's sweetness. It was a wonder the Skaialan had any teeth left. "I came here to warn ye, and to give ye whatever gold ye need to make your way South again."

"Two hundred pieces of Northern gold, perhaps?" I supplied, helpfully. "With a wolf-rune stamped on each?"

"Tis what my life seems to be worth here." Redfist glowered, but his color had returned to what passed for normal. His hands were still fists, but I judged him not likely to use them at the moment. "Well, now ye've seen me, Emrath, and ye may take yerself north to yer husband's Keep. I hear he built thee a fine one."

"Did ye think I'd simply sit and wait?" The giantess took two steps away from the fireplace, halted, and rounded on him with another sway of her skirts, her overshoes clop-grinding the carpet. "Let my clan follow the Redfist into the underworld, bairn to brawn? I had no *choice*, Rainak!"

Redfist folded his brawny arms across his barrel chest. "Ye could have come with me."

"Oh, aye, and leave Kalburn to fire and rapine." Emrath rolled her grey eyes like a young girl at her first Festival. "Would that have pleased thee?"

Mother Moon. D'ri rose, paced to the window, his

voice-within shot through with sardonic amusement. *We traveled through ice, harpies, and bandits for a lover's quarrel.*

My agreement took the form of a half-swallowed laugh, but I did not move from the door. No sounds untoward sounds in the hallway, yet. If we had to make a quick escape, could we reach the stables in time? The prospect of a gallop with restive stolen *torkascruagh*—if this woman's escort had not a man or two posted in the stable now to deny us escape—and traveling along the bandit-infested road again with just our three blades and whatever provision we could take from our attackers was not a pleasant one.

"You know it would not." Redfist stepped toward her, once, twice. He did not wish to, that much was plain, but was clearly unable to halt. All the beads had left his great ruddy beard. He had sloughed the south as easily as I would push this place form my skin, did it please the gods to return me to civilization whole.

I had never seen our barbarian act thus towards a woman, even lovely Kesamine, my Clau darling of the Swallow's Moon. Which gave me much food for thought, when I could spare a moment or two for it.

"Then take what I can give ye, Rainak Redfist, and go south again." She gathered the front of her cloak, crushing and smoothing folds in turn. "And *live*. Tis the only thing that made *this* bearable, the thought that you were free, living out of his cursed reach."

"Free as a beggar, oh, indeed. Free as a starving dog." Redfist's hands dropped to his sides, beginning to open and close, and I wondered if he felt her throat against his palms. "You did not send Corran Ninefinger to me, then? With a lock of your golden hair?"

"Corran…" A number of expressions traversed her face, swift as startled marshbirds, and D'ri turned from the window, his dark gaze meeting mine. "I knew he had escaped, but—"

"He carried Northern gold and a sealed commission to assassins in Antai." It was a day for me to be singularly helpful in conversation, apparently. "Friend Redfist, I like not the way this caravan is wending."

"Assassins…" She all but staggered under the news. Her shoulder hit the mantel, a heavy bruising blow, and Redfist moved as if to help her, but she retreated from his grasp.

I did not blame her.

"Kaia." Darik had turned back to the window. "You should see this."

There was still no sound in the hallway, and the commonroom's rumble below the floorboards held no note of approaching violence. I eased away from the door with a sigh, setting my mug upon the table. Redfist nodded, prompting the woman to go on.

She swallowed, hard. If she was lying, no doubt she needed to wet her throat. "Corran came from the North an eightmoon ago. He begged me to help him escape. I made certain he could leave through Karnaugh. He said he would find you and tell you…tell you what I meant you to hear."

I arrived at D'ri's side, peering through the small porthole that passed for a window. It showed a slice of frost-rimed cobblestone street below, a corner that should have held a bard, a holysinger, or perhaps a player or two performing for bits of leftover Skaialan copper tradewire in the thin gray morning light. Instead, it was bare, except for two hefty Skaialan giants in patterned blue cloth that matched the woman's skirts.

"Two guards," I said, in tradetongue peppered

with Shainakh instead of Skaialan. "Wearing skirts to match hers, Redfist."

"Of course, the lady of Kalburn doesnae go into a common inn without a heavy hand or two about." Redfist drew himself up, switching to Skaialan, the words thrumming in his chest. "I am bound for the Standing Stones, Emrath Needleslay, and I will challenge your husband. Corran led me to believe you wished as much."

"No, you blundering oaf, I wish for you to live." She gathered her skirts in both hands. "Please, Rainak. I can give you a fast *treikaull* and guards—"

"I do not like this," I interrupted. "She has all but announced us to the entire city."

"Shut your mouth, foreign whore." Sharp and disdainful, Emrath spat the last term at me with a measure of icy contempt.

Do they know no other insult? It was puzzling, and they pronounced it as if those who slake the desires of the flesh for coin are somewhat unclean. Even the Pesh are not so venomous, though they hold females to be only receptive vessels for any male, god or beast, to use as they please. A female sellsword in Pesh is a rare article, likely fast and deadly to escape the coffle.

I should know.

A short sharp crack echoed against the walls, the two sturdy beds—both of them large enough for two G'mai or a single Skaialan giant—and the small table where Darik's scraped-empty bowl and my cooling mug stood sentinel. I turned from the window to see the fair-haired giantess with a sting-reddened cheek, and Rainak Redfist lowering a bladed hand as he spoke, even quiet words that nonetheless managed to chill more than the sleet outside. "K'ai Iron-Flower is *wal'kir*, she is a shieldmaiden of Kroth Himself, and ye will not insult her again, Emrath Needleslay."

I forgave him much in that moment. Perhaps I should not have, for a man who strikes one woman will strike another. I peered again out the window, taking in what I could of the men on the corner. They did not seem happy to be standing in the sleet, but they were not glancing up at the inn windows, nor were they paying much attention to the passers-by. I could perhaps knock out the glass and slide through the aperture, but D'ri's shoulders were too broad, and Redfist...well, squeezing him through like a pet Shainakh longrat sent down a snake-burrow was an amusing thought, but not even close to possible. "Redfist?" I did not need to add the rest of the question. *Do we move now? And do we leave the woman alive?*

My barbarian friend stared at the woman, her cheek now stained vivid crimson. She regarded him fiercely, unblinking, and the two of them seemed well-matched indeed.

"My apologies," Emrath Needleslay said, colorlessly. Her stance did not relax, tight as a lutestring, and she did not so much as glance at me. "Do you be my guest tonight, Rainak Redfist, and your two elvish sprites as well. I am still Lady of Kalburn; even my husband cannot kill you there." Her chin rose a fraction. "He is due from the North soon, to attempt the calling of the Clans to the Standing Stones." Her gaze had become remote, chill as ice-flowers upon their fine glass windows. "Tomorrow you may, if you wish to, call them first."

A GUEST IS SACRED

THE SKAIALAN CALL IT *OGIDAUGH*; the word in G'mai is *hal'adai'ara*. To the Shainakh it is *ka-atet*, the Hain have their own all-but-unpronounceable term. So, and so on. A household guest in all those lands is sacred, and may not be harmed unless one wishes to draw down the wrath of things older than gods. In the Highlands, it is not even the mother of Kroth who punishes transgressors, but her *three* mothers— the ones who gave parts of their bodies to make the spines of the mountains, the eyes of the Sun and Moon, and the belly of all-giving earth.

I wondered if Corran Ninefinger had complained bitterly to them as he staggered bruised and bloody through Antai's cobbled streets, and if we were likely to meet a similar fate in Kalburn.

Needleslay rode in a *treikaull*, a manner of sled with three greased runners, pulled by a pair of *torkascruagh* bred for speed and consequently smaller than most. The beasts had white patches along their sides, as if singed, and the sled was full of furs and soft materials. She had invited me to ride within it as well, but I declined with a single glance. Instead, our trio rode *torkascruagh* borrowed from her guards, who had to trudge back to their duties afoot.

If she wanted to alert the entire Highlands to Redfist's presence, she was doing a fine job of it. And Redfist, the great gingery gruel-brained barbarian, seemed content to let her do so. I mulled this at length, fixing each turn of Kalburn's winding streets in my head as I would the lay of a battlefield. There was one thing that cheered me—the roofs inside the city's thick, ancient walls, though steeply pitched, were crammed so close together a *torkascruagh* could ride across them with a little luck.

A much smaller G'mai accustomed to thievery and slippery footing would have an easier time.

The citadel of Kalburn rose, a high, thin block of stone thrusting from Highland earth. By *block* I mean it was all of a piece, not built, not held together by mortar. A narrow mountain-tooth, worn almost to the gums by time and wind but still larger than petty human concerns. Its rooms were *carved* instead of constructed. There were timber and stone outbuildings, but the citadel itself was where Needleslay slept and held her board, and also where she sat in a cold high-ceilinged room upon a dais and a low bench likewise chipped from the solid stone, all in one piece, to hear arguments presented by those of her clan in some suit or dispute.

It reminded me of Anjalismir, and that made me uneasy. Redfist's acceptance of her hospitality made me uneasy as well. A blade in the dark I may handily fight but poisons are not my specialty, and it is easy enough to add such things to a guest's food, especially when a guest is a man who has struck you open-handed. I am a sellsword worth good red Shainakh gold, and a *s'tarei* is nothing to discount either, but enough numbers can overwhelm even the mightiest.

These pleasant musings accompanied us all the way through the citadel's outbuildings, the five-sided fenced spaces for sparring or dueling—the Skaialan do not duel under a roof, believing it bad form. Kroth must be able to witness their battles, for little delights him more than honorable bloodshed, this hungry Northern god.

Under a dark, heavy sky and the iron tang of more wet snow about to heave itself from Kroth's cellars, we were formally welcomed to Kalburn's citadel. A double-handled cup of beaten metal was brought, and standing uon the steps before great doors of scarred and iron-bound timber, the fair-haired giantess drank a healthy draft and passed it to Redfist. He accepted with both hands, hefted the brassy metal, and took a long swallow.

I glanced at the onlookers—dour Skaialan giants with hair ruddy, gold, or dark, their naked, furry calves spattered with mud and snowmelt, the guards in skirts that matched the pattern upon Needleslay's. Above, heavy shutters closed over most windows, but a few in sheltered places were uncapped, full of pale smears. I later learned they were the women-servants and children watching the arrival of guests, excited and agog.

Redfist handed the cup to me. The thing was as wide across as my forearm is long, and the liquid within steamed fragrant with spice and alcohol. I took a cautious sniff—wine, with sweet herbs.

My hesitation might have been insulting. I met the Skaialan woman's pale gaze, the skin between my shoulderblades roughening instinctively.

I lifted the cauldron-thing to my lips with no little effort, and took a sip. Passed it to D'ri with a nod, and he copied me, barely wetting his lips. That was apparently enough to appease custom, and from that moment we were the witnessed guests of the woman Northerners called the Keeper of the Stones, the only woman who commanded fighting men in the whole of the Highlands.

I MIGHT ALMOST HAVE LIKED her, if not for what was to come.

A DEEPWYRM'S EYES

A Skaialan high feast is rather like a Shainakh army camp. There is smoke, both from fires and from pipes carved from *torkascruagh* horn and stuffed with bogweed, smoked to ease the lungs and sharpen the appetite. There is meat, roasting upon spits in the high hearth or carried from great clamoring smoke-hell kitchens, and there is liquor. Mead, both mash and distilled, and deep harsh ale that must be watered, and for the children, bubbling thick small-ale and sofin. Roasted meatroot, pasties, all manner of different spices and scents crowding the nose, fighting with the fume of smoke and inebriation. The pressure of a crowd, shoulder to shoulder, hip to hip, elbows rubbing as they consume.

Most of all, though, there is the *noise*, fair to shake the carven stone and timber roof down upon us. Toasts called across the room, drunken altercations settled with blows or by the crowd pulling two combatants apart, children shrieking with joy as they ran from table to table, sampling at will. From the raised end of the room where the lord or commander sits, all this can be surveyed and the crowd is somewhat less, and as the lady's personal guests, we were treated to the spectacle and only half-deafened by it.

Oiled, scraped, baked in the heat of their strange little *skauna*-rooms and with my hair freshly braided, D'ri similarly bathed and both of us in jerkin-and-trews, we must have been a strange sight to the Northerners, to judge by the staring. Of course, we were armed, and that had almost been a problem until Redfist explained that our ways required it in order to defend our host's honor if necessary. It was an inspired bit of silvertongue explanation, one I had no idea lurked inside his barbarian skull.

Those who did not study the strange southroners watched him, for he was a sight indeed.

I had to admit, dressed like his fellow countrymen, Rainak Redfist was an imposing figure. His skirt was a different color and pattern than the Needleslay and her guards', and there had been a rippling hush when he strode into the dining-hall after her, D'ri and I gliding ghosts in his wake. With his hair clubbed afresh and his beard and moustache no longer oiled and beaded but rough-combed into a torrent, a wide creaking-new leather belt holding his skirt fastened and the excess material drawn up and flung over his left shoulder, he moved just as his fellow giants did. No longer was he an uncertain mass of man in too-small buildings, clumsily handling eating picks and almost breaking every chair. He sat at the Needleslay's right, and their heads bent together during the meal. Deep in conversation, Redfist did not even glance at me.

I watched the crowd, as D'ri murmured an occasional comment in my ear. We could guess who held high rank and who held low, and there were a few who looked a bit green at Redfist's appearance. Children pointed at me and giggled, ran to the foot of the

dais and eyed me to test their courage. Fighting men
—the Needleslay's guard, all with a crescent-brooch
of silver stabbed by a short bar—examined us as well.
One in particular, a black-bearded giant, watched me
as if he expected me to shed my usual form and turn
into a tree-viper. He chewed slowly, and his coal-
dark eyes were thoughtful and wary.

That one could be troublesome. Often the quiet ones
are stupid, but sometimes they are simply thoughtful,
and woe to the sellsword who doesn't grasp the difference.

"The merriment here has an edge," D'ri said,
softly.

I nodded. There was a strangeness about the
laughter, fey and unwholesome. As far as I could tell,
the food held no poison, but I did not trust the ale.
There were women huddled near the great fireplaces
attending the meat, fear in their quick glances but
defiance in the set of their pale, uncooked-dough
shoulders. Many of the men grew more nervous as
the feast progressed. A few drank to sotting and slid
off their benches, landing with shattering thumps on
the flags scattered with sweetstraw and rushes.

They are expecting something dreadful. I glanced at
Redfist, still engrossed with the golden-headed head
giantess. Instinct itched along my back and upper
arms, reaching such a pitch I stood, scraping my
heavy wooden chair back with a squeal, as a door at
the other end of the hall slid silently open.

The new arrival wore dark clothing, the long
cloth serving as both skirt and sash holding no colorful linear patterns like every other man's. His
blousy shirt was dark too, and his belt was broad
oiled leather.

My *s'tarei*'s hand closed, warm and hard, around
my wrist.

Once, early in our travels together, he had grasped my ankle, and his intent was the same now—to fill me with Power, should there be need. Just as any *s'tarei* would, with his *adai*. Perhaps it looked to others as if he held me back from loosing steel. A cold, scaled creeping of something loathsome flicked over my skin, rasping against the borders of mind and body Janaire and the *taih'adai* had taught me to erect. The new arrival had some measure of Power, a clumsy childish use of what the G'mai call the Moon's gifts.

The Skaialan, no doubt, could sense it too.

It was not the man's hair, a dim shade between blond and brown. After so many bearded faces, it was somewhat of a shock to see pale, scraped cheeks. He wore no blush from the cold, either.

No, it was the film over his eyes, a pale spider-webbing over deep darkness that was not how eyes should look. They were like a deepwyrm's clouded orbs, but *those* beasts bear such a gaze naturally, for night-fighting in their caverns. They rarely surface, and then, only at night for mating. This man had a deepwyrm's eyes, and the set of his broad meaty shoulders was wrong as well. The angle was strange, as if something fluid had run into his bones and twisted them a bare fraction.

His appearance was cold barqa-slops thrown upon a fire to kill its glow. A chill breeze mouthed the hall, Power stirring, spreading like dark oil.

He showed his filed-sharp teeth, this newcomer, and a cringing went through the proud Northerners. On the grass sea of the Danhai plains, some do such things to their mouths. It gives their opponents pause there, as well.

The women at the fire drew closer together, the children scattered to find shelter against adults. The fighting men blanched, and the only sound was Redfist's booming, brassy voice, ricocheting from every carven edge. "And what's this, now? A blind man?"

In Hain, the pause in a crowd's babble is attributed to one of their many gods or almost-gods passing feather-light through the room. Those whose voices break it by chance are held to be of special interest to the god in question, and must visit a temple to divine which they may have offended or honored. The long quiet here held a similar quality; there was a scramble of motion—all the serving-folk retreating with shushing, hurried steps for the door to the kitchens. This left only those trapped at the dais, one serving-girl passing me with a sharp inhaled breath, as if she wished to hide behind my chair.

The newcomer tilted his head. "Who speaks?" he said, quietly, and a shocking warm tenor came slowly from that serrated, too-loose mouth.

A ponderous scraping was Redfist's chair, its high-pointed back quivering slightly, pushed back along the floor of the stone dais. My hand dropped to a knifehilt—not my largest knife, and not my smallest, but the one near the middle on the light side.

The one best for throwing.

"Rainak," I said quietly, in tradetongue though my mouth longed for G'mai, "this one has some witchery upon him."

"Give me your name, blind man." Redfist's voice swallowed the last of my sentence, pitched to carry and cover my warning. "And I shall give you mine."

A hideous scraping chuckle misused the newcomer's soft tenor. I *felt* the witchery-creature prepare to move in my own knees, ankles, elbows, every string of muscle I possessed.

My wrist tore free of Darik's grip as I hopped back and *up*, fish-lunging, bootsoles catching my chair's thin horsehair cushion. I would have leapt from there to the table, had not Darik surged to his feet and thrown his arm about my waist, knocking me sideways. We landed on Emrath Needleslay, her chair's arm striking my knee with a sound like wet wood chopped in half, and a faint floral scent mixed with the musk of a large woman who did not soak in hot water when she could swallowed me. The giantess slid from her chair with a strangled yelp that might have been amusing had it not been cracked halfway by my skull hitting her shoulder, and we went down in a tangle. Stunned, I sprawled atop her, both of us under the table in a chaos of arms and legs.

A whistling, a thump, a high drilling noise through my skull that chose not to pour through my ears first. A heatless scent I knew well—battle, and blood drawn. D'ri, having shoved me atop the Needleslay and gained his feet with unthinking, battle-mad grace, launched himself, his boot-toe grabbing a slice of tabletop and the entire great wooden thing rocking as he soared. He hit the wyrm-eyed man in midair, a collision strangely free of noise, and I only knew afterward because the Skaialan spoke of it in hushed whispers.

Like one of the great drakes he flew, that one. They know of wingwyrms in the cold North, as well.

Redfist bellowed, a sound I knew well from many a battlefield, and my hands sank into Emrath Needleslay's capacious bosom as I thrashed to free myself and be of some use against whatever witch-thing this was.

When I gained my feet, all I saw was the thing on the floor twitching, foulness sliding from beneath its dark skirts as it hissed its dying throes. Redfist stared at it, his mouth drawn tight, and Darik made a sharp economical movement, wrenching one of his *dotanii* free of muscle suction. *"Al'adai ma'adaiina reshai,"* he murmured, and I found my own lips moving as he said it.

Mother Moon, in defense of my twin. One of the traditional prayers, uttered by a *s'tarei* who had just killed to protect his *adai.*

I let out a soft, shuddering sigh. Redfist, his meaty fists up, stood prepared to defend himself. The body kept twitching, and the stink that rose from it was not the honest stench of loosed bowels.

"He killed a Black Brother," someone said, low and clearly, in Skaialan. It was the black-bearded, quiet man. He gazed at my *s'tarei* as if seeing a Festival puppet perform something new and wondrous.

There was a general motion for the doors, and the feast, it seemed, was over.

OTHER THAN I WAS

In a small circular room high in one of Kalburn Keep's towers a tapestry loom gathered dust, the strands upon it faded and damp. A good fire had been laid and a flagon of strong mead brought, but I only took advantage of the former.

"Witchery indeed," Redfist said grimly, resting his chin on his broad hand. The fire snapped as it consumed its blackrock fuel with filthy smoke, and I kept my arms folded tight lest a shiver running through my hands betray me. The warming breath would not come; I was too busy holding my entire body still, so the shaking could not be seen.

"They are now his black brothers." Emrath Needleslay outright hugged herself, elbows cupped in her soft white palms. "It used to be simply his Guard were named thus as a mark of honor, but now... Some go to him to be sworn, and they return like *that*. Hollowed out." She cast a nervous glance at me, no doubt because she thought I had thrown myself upon her to guard her life.

I did not bother to disabuse her of the notion. Nor did I take my *s'tarei* to task for tossing me into a giantess's bosom. Darik paced quietly to the door, made a half-turn, and paced to the hole in the wall masquerading as a window. It was thickly glassed, and it had iced over completely upon its outside.

"Hollowed out?" I repeated in tradetongue, wanting to make very sure I had translated the Ska-ialan correctly.

"Do you know of such things?" Redfist's gaze was turned fully on me now, for perhaps the first time since we had arrived at Kalburn. "Your people...well, J'na..."

Janaire would probably be of more use. And yet, how quickly our barbarian turned to me once more, after all but ignoring me as his countrymen did their own women. "There are tales of such things," I admitted. "To frighten children."

"Kaia." Darik did not stop pacing, but he spoke rapidly in G'mai, his inflection precise and sharp as a warmaster laying out tactics for a student. "A black use of Power indeed; is he accusing you of such things?"

"Not me, *s'tarei'mi.*" I freed a hand, pinched the bridge of my nose as if it would give me an answer to this riddle. "And we shall speak of you tossing me into that woman's tits before long." Deliberately crude, the inflection that of a student addressing an-other on equal terms.

His even pace faltered for a half-moment, then carried on.

"What does he say?" Redfist wanted to know.

"One moment, my large friend." The Skaialan fit awkwardly in my mouth after G'mai's liquid cadence. I inhaled deeply, the warming breath igniting low in my belly. Let the air out softly, drew it in to fuel that glow.

"Do the elvish know of such things?" Needleslay addressed herself to Redfist, and my dislike of her sharpened, if that were possible. Mother *Moon*, I hate that word. They use it to mean *different*, and *strange*, and it is only a hairsbreadth after using it they decide that what is strange is dangerous.

And must be killed.

"D'ri, have you heard of this?" I pinched my nose a little harder, as if the pressure could untangle what I had just seen and force it into sense. The half-done tapestry sagging upon the loom bothered me, too. "I left G'maihallan so young, all I can remember are some bits of the greater Lay of Belariaa. They speak of the dark that came, but…I do not know." I was never one to stay with the Yada'Adais, preferring the practice ground despite all her gentle urging. A child's misunderstanding of her attempt to show me the Power stirring around other girl-children, and it had led me through years and battles to precisely *here*.

It was enough to make even a sellsword wonder at the ways of gods, and…fate? Was that the word? The Hain hold that none can alter theirs, written in a great book and held by one of their many gods.

My *s'tarei* kept pacing, his strides the even drops of a water-clock. "*Sharauq'belios*," he said, shortly.

Of all the words in my native tongue, he had to choose one I did not know, and with a short, crisp inflection that gave me no clue. It meant *foul glove*, if one took it child-literally, but the root *sharauq'ar* is a filth that will not wash away, a stain that cannot be erased. "Darikaan." I may have even said it sharply, with the extra twist at the end that made him into a balky mount. "An explanation would be much appreciated by your *adai*."

That brought him round upon his heel, his boot grinding into the floor—timber for this room, not stone, and I was glad of it. Too much rock will bruise the feet, even through the best boots, and this cold, dirty place full of mannerless giants did not make it softer.

He almost glared at me, his eyes dark coals. "We should leave this place at once, *adai'mi*. I have little hope that you will see reason."

"Difficult to set forth, in this weather." I dropped my hand, since pinching the bridge of my nose did not make my looming headache recede. Shook my arms out, as the warming breath cycled through me again. It was impossible to deny the steadying effect of his mere presence, a luxury I had missed all my life. "Tell me of the foul glove."

"What is he *saying*?" Redfist smacked the arm of his chair with a clenched fist, a dull, thudding sound. *He* was not troubled by the tapestry upon the loom or by Emrath Needleslay's trembling. "If you know what *that thing* was—"

That brought my gaze to rest upon him, and Darik's as well. I spoke for us both, and sharply, too. "He is in the process of explaining, my barbarian friend." Their word for *foreigner* is suspiciously full of sibilants; I might almost suspect it kin to the Shainakh term for a money-grubbing swine. "Try not to interrupt."

"Rainak." Needleslay stiffened, her pale eyes round and a splatter of roast-grease upon the cuff of her fine satin sleeve. "That elvish *bint* speaks to ye thus?"

My right hand ached for my *dotani*'s hilt, an almost physical pain. But Redfist shook his head, settling back into the chair. I began to think perhaps his legs were not as steady as he liked to pretend, and such a thing should not have cheered me.

Yet it did.

"Yes, Emrath." Redfist spread his hand, no longer

a hard fist but loose fingers, surprisingly delicate for their size. "K'ai the Steelflower speaks as she pleases, to me."

With that settled, I waited for Darik. Still glaring, still every fingerwidth the Dragaemir princeling, though his travel-gear was more worn than I liked and the fur jerkin after the Northern pattern made him seem leaner than he was. Or perhaps it appeared so because the cold of the Pass will melt flesh from even a *s'tarei* trained by the finest warmasters of my people, and the country's inhabitants with their ill-humor and terrible food do not help.

Darik looked as if he were weighing two uncomfortable truths, and seeking to find a balance between them. *Lita arauq'idin*, we call it, the hesitation between rocks and whirlpool. "There are...scrolls. In the Palace, meant for a *s'tarei*'s education." He stood, tense-shouldered, braced for battle. "Of the many illnesses Power may wreak among the lesser of the world. Such things are necessary to know of, so one may guard against."

I nodded. "And the *foul glove*?" *The tapestry is Emrath's*, I realized, with a sudden deep certainty. No doubt she had been called away from her work years ago, and had not returned.

"It takes much Power, Kaia. To pour something filthy-black-whole into a man, so *something else* sees through his eyes. The victim is left without a will of his own, an empty vessel, and lives only to serve its master. They are...bloodthirsty." Darik used the word for animals with the water-sickness, foaming and suffering, not caring what or whom they bite. He had paled under his even coppery coloring, for to speak of such a misuse of Power is a dreadful obscenity. The Moon would turn Her face from one who practiced it in my faraway homeland, and a deep unsteadiness gripped my stomach. "There are ways to do so. No *adai* would ever...and yet, Power itself carries the tale of what is possible, so we know."

"An empty vessel," I repeated slowly, in tradetongue. The nausea did not subside. The idea of stealing away another's *self*...even the best and most hardened of thieves might well shudder at the prospect. You could take a target's jewels, their standing, their freedom, even their life, but to take what should always remain inviolable, the most secret inner hollows within their chest, their eyes, their head-meat? No. Such a thing was foul indeed. "A man witched away from his own will, another seeing through his eyes."

"So ye do know of such things." Redfist let out a long sigh. "Dunkast, my brother...What did he find, in the North? He changed after the battle with the blue tribes, but it was never this..."

He plainly did not expect an answer, but one arrived nonetheless.

"A great greenmetal chain, with a black gem." Emrath surprised us all. "He wears it openly now, about his shoulders like a steward of some great office." She had paled alarmingly even for her kind, blue veinmaps standing out under her skin.

Redfist did not look at her, but his tone sharpened. "Did you see that on the wedding night?"

"He hasnae touched me, Redfist Rainak. I did not let him." Haughty, her chin rose, her pale braids moving against her dress. "The marriage is only *convenience*. A *talanach*."

I did not know the word; I did not bother to ask its meaning. Redfist did not look in the mood to give me a lesson in its use.

"A gem?" Darik's accent turned the word sideways

in tradetongue; he had not taken to Skaialan as I had. "Upon a chain?"

"They say the metal is turning to stone." Emrath Needleslay's shudder rippled all the way through her skirt, and Redfist finally rose.

"Come now." Gentle, as he would with a maddened or shivering mount. "Sit, *corra-luagnh*."

"I had to." She gazed up at him, those pale eyes brimful with salt water. "He did not want *me*, Rainak. He only wanted Kalburn, and I gave him what I could to keep my people safe." She sank into the chair with a sigh, and it did not creak as it accepted her. Her skirts fell in long, flowing drapes, masking her legs and inhibiting both flight and fighting.

No doubt if I were a proper G'mai woman I would be wearing something similar, and I would allow my *s'tarei* to take me from this hideous place. If I were a proper G'mai woman I would never have left my home, believing I was the only of my kind to walk alone. I would never have made my living as a sellsword traveling the Rim, and never have picked a giant's pocket in a Hain tavern.

But I had done all those things, and they had led me step by step to the white wastes and this block of stone housing treachery, black sorcery, and giant boar. Were I more religious, I might well think I had angered a god or two—or amused one.

"I like this talk of a gem even less." Darik regarded me, evenly. Perhaps he could tell the direction my thoughts were tending. "I do not wish to risk you here, Kaia. The things they speak of, the thing in the hall—they may consume an *adai*."

Consume. He used the word for a shoat swallowed whole by a wingwyrm, a truly unpleasant feat. I let the warming breath cycle through me once more, twice. It helped. "Steel should guard against such witchery."

"And you shall have mine." There it was again, the play on words, the allusion to the more *intimate* aspects of the twin-bond. His eyebrow did not rise, nor did he smile, but it was no doubt close.

I tipped my head back, rolled it left and right to dispel some of the aching. It did not help. There was no soothing to be found in this conversation, and I suspected it would turn even less pleasant before long.

I was not disappointed. "Durran." Redfist had turned grave, his mouth vanishing into his beard, and the burr in his tradetongue mangled D'ri's name. "I know that look of yours."

"I am asking her to leave this place." Darik's quiet gravity was unaltered by tradetongue. Bladed cheek-bones stood out, harsh mountain-bones to rival those upon the horizon, taking their stark beauty from G'-maihallan. "Those things are dangerous to our women."

I bit my lip, rolled my head a little more. My headache intensified instead of easing, of course. Once pain settles in the skull, it is not easily routed.

The quality of their silence warned me. I brought my chin back down and caught the subtle flickers in their expressions—men, reaching an understanding without words. They think being born without a trouser-string means women cannot decipher such looks.

"A fast sled, and guards." Redfist straightened, and his palm cupped the Needleslay's shoulder, polishing it with a soft, absent motion. She sagged, as if a weight had been taken from her. "Ye may take Kaia back to Antai, and—"

"There will be no taking me *anywhere*, thank you."

I focused on the warming breath, inhaling smoothly, tapping my body's small fires to echo the larger one crackle-eating its fuel to warm the room. "You may treat your women as cattle here, Redfist, but *I* am not to be herded."

"I knew you would not see reason," D'ri murmured. But softly, and his mind was a closed fist, an internal withdrawing. We gave each other what privacy we could, within the twinbond.

Or, more precisely, he gave me the distance I needed, and I gave him all the closeness I could stand.

Well enough. If I were less tired, I might have told him of a certain village in the Pesh borderlands, of a deep foul thing hiding in a cave, and the look on wan villagers' faces when I brought the unnatural *thing's* misshapen, dripping head to their fear-fueled bonfire one balmy spring night, avenging their missing children.

They had not been grateful for long, those tillers of thin soil, but by the time their welcome began to fade, I was already gone.

"Redfist." I grasped firmly at my patience, thinning rapidly with each day in this icy hell. At least in Antai these two had not harassed me so. "Are you telling me you no longer wish my sword at your back?" My tradetongue, salted deeply with Skaialan, was an unhappy sound at best.

The ruddy giant opened his mouth, and I thought he would say, *yes, that is what I am telling you, lass, now begone with your elvish princeling.* Instead, the barbarian coughed, and Darik's eyes narrowed, reading the terrain as a strategist might.

"I…lass, you are welcome with me, as long as you choose to stay." Rainak Redfist coughed again. Perhaps more words were crowding his throat, unable to struggle free. "But you should listen to your *corjhan* there."

"I hear both of you perfectly well." With that, I strode for the door, each footstep brittle as the hold I had on my temper.

I could not blame my childhood Yada'Adais, or the Moon, or any other god. I, and I alone, had set myself upon this road.

It was too late now to pretend to be other than I was.

NO UNLEARNING

I DO NOT KNOW where Darik slept that night; he did not return to the cold, cavernous room given over to our use. Nor did Redfist, but *that* did not bother me much.

What did were the dreams, treading the same groove in my sleeping, over and over again like a pacing beast.

I CHARGED. Not straight for them—though that would have been satisfying—but to the left, where the shadows were deepest. Boots stamping, my legs complaining, ice underfoot and my left knee threatening to buckle again before silence descended upon me. It was not the killing snow-quiet I had discovered after my mother's death, but the white-hot clarity of battlerage. There is a moment, when the body has been pushed past endurance and your enemies are still all about you, when the last reserves inside a sellsword—those crockery jars full of burn-the-mouth, sweetheavy turit *jam—are smashed. Muscle may pull from bone, bone may break, but the sellsword will not feel it for hours. The Shainakh call it* nahrappan, *the Hain a*

term that has to do with a cornered animal, and in G'mai it is called the s'tarei's last kiss, and it is said that even after an adai's death a s'tarei may perform one last action, laying waste to his opponents.

The Skaialan call it berserk, and there are tales of their warriors fighting naked except for crimson chalk-paint, touched by Kroth's heavy hand and driven mad.

Pain vanished. My dotani clove frozen air with a low sweet sound, blurring in a low arc as I turned sideways, skipping from cobble to cobble with no grace but a great deal of speed. The far-left Black Brother had an axe, and all thought left me as it moved, hefted as if it weighed less than a straw. Their soft, collective grasping burned away, I left the ground and flew, turning at the last moment, the arc halting and cutting down, sinking through fur and leather, snap-grinding on bone, and the Black Brother's mouth opened wet-loose as his arm separated, neatly cloven. The axe, its momentum inescapable, sheared to the side, and since his left hand was the brace for the haft it arced neatly into his next-door compatriot, sinking in with the heavy sound of well-seasoned wood.

Their child-high screams rose, but I was already past, and Mother Moon, I longed to turn back. The burning in my veins, the sweet-hot rage, demanded it.

Instead, I put my head down and bolted. Thump-thud, thump-thud, the street familiar now, each shadow turning bright-sharp as my pupils swelled, the taste in my mouth sour copper and katai candy. The Keep loomed ever closer, and if I could reach the end there was a narrow housefront with a door left deliberately unlocked. Once inside, I could be up the stairs and out a high window, onto the roof-road again, up and down while the foul glove-net closed on empty air. There was an easy way into the Keep from there, if D'ri had reached it and secured the knotted rope...

A whistle-crunch. Another high childlike cry behind me as a heavy black-fletched arrow, its curve aimed high

and sharp to give it added force as it fell, pierced a pursuer's skull, shattering it in a spray of bone and grey
matter.

Kaia! *Thin and very far away, struggling to reach me
through the rage.* Kaia, down!

My feet tangled in an invisible skein, and I fell...

∾

ONCE, twice, however many times I woke in that
room, the low keening of a Skaialan wind restlessly
mouthed the walls. The fire turned to blackrock
coals, my breath became visible, and I burrowed into
the bed, curling around myself like a hibernating
creature. A *moro* of the G'mai mountains, or a Clau
laihanaura, the toads that sleep in mud waiting for
their rainy season to come again. Candlemarks
passed, and when the faint gray light of morning slid
past the iron-bound windows and the heavy drapes
covering them, I was well on my way to cursing
every snow-god I had ever heard of, and every soul in
the Highlands as well.

At least the privies were not *outside*, here. That is a
measure of luxury in their part of the world; perhaps
that is why Redfist and his fellows are so hairy. They
need pelts in order not to freeze to death while re-
lieving themselves in the late watches. I made my
way through the passages, halting whenever a fit of
shivering threatened to take my legs from me. I
avoided the sight and sound of others—they blundered through the halls with little stealth, these Skaialan giants. Movement dispelled some of the cold,
the warming breath finally drove it from my arms
and legs, and the pattern of Kalburn's great keep was
not difficult to pierce.

Even my traveling-cloak, fur-lined and vast

enough to swallow me since it was cut for a giantess and only lately trimmed, was inadequate. It took a great deal of effort to nerve myself to it, but I finally worked my way outside, into an ice-rimed bailey with frowning walls. My ears twitched, and it took me a half-candlemark to find what I sought.

The warriors of Skaialan practice their art in all weather, as any worth their steel must. Their dueling-grounds are not round but five-cornered, each point marked with cardinal pillars, open to the sky so Kroth may witness all. I did not wish a duel, I simply wanted the training-yard, and found one. Flail, pike, shield, their massive straight swords— meant for hacking, not slashing, grace, or speed— and double-bladed axes, the single-axes always used in pairs, for knifework considered below a warrior's dignity. A sellsword, ever alert to new technique or a subtle skill, may learn much by simply watching.

I did not wish *that*, either.

Instead, I chose a corner of their five-pointed beaten-earth space empty enough for my purposes, closed my eyes, and breathed deep. Cold like a meat-knife stinging throat and nose, the clash-slither of blades or thocking of weighted wood, grunts and curses and foul exhalations.

Yes. This was, as far as I could find in this hideous place, a familiar comfort. If I have anything resembling home in the wide wide world, it is where I hear the sounds of those who train for combat.

My hand closed about my *dotani* hilt, swept the blade free with its familiar, welcoming sound. I began with the simplest of forms, holding each stroke for a moment, warming and loosening. The cloak was a hindrance, but worse was the squashing slop of ice upon dirt and scattered straw underfoot.

Flagged stone, even with scattered hay or rushes or dirt to provide traction, is not ideal.

The first strokes—piri-splitter, sidesweep, hilt floating up, stab and retreat, turn with the forefoot down and the heel light—unreeled. The warming breath came more easily; my shivers eased. When I had warmed enough I shrugged from the cloak and tossed it over a rack of weighted wooden practice-maces, probably dragged outside each day by trainees. My ear-tips were numb even in a nest of braids, dressed winter-fashion about the head to conserve what heat I could.

Star-strike once, twice, again. Blurring into the third of the Great Forms, the most challenging. The minstrel's plea, the losing toss, I drew my largest knife, my fingers unwieldy but still answering my will, and flowed into other forms. Moves learned in the Shainakh irregulars, playing out old duels or battles still echoing in my flesh—the body does not forget. It is *made* to remember, with training, and once it learns that trick there is no unlearning.

Even if you wish it. Even if you long to be other than what you are. What you have made yourself.

Breath hard and sharp, blood pumping, the cold no longer vicious but clear Karun white wine sparkling into my throat, filling my heaving lungs with starlight. I began to work in earnest then, foot stamping at the strike-moment, a *kia-ah* escaping me at a particularly vicious blow.

It was Danhai I thought of, the cursed plains in winter. Summers were for campaigning, but when the screaming ice-rimed winds came across the great grass sea there was nothing but dicing, stealth-raids, and the perpetual quest to keep warm. I had thought, then, that the Danhai must be at least part ice-demon. Now, perhaps, I knew what true cold was, and it was not to be found even in the Highlands, no matter how their white winds wailed.

There is nothing as chilling as measuring yourself —and finding a lack.

Stamp-shuffle, blurring across a memory-field, turning as an invisible arrow whistled past—that was at night, just before the spring rains turned any track on the Plains into a quagmire of sucking black mud. A stealth-raid with Ammerdahl Rikyat, and our small cadre running across a similarly tiny party of Danhai out to cause mischief. The sound of a bowstring travels differently, at night.

So do the cries of the dying.

My luck will turn against me, Kaia!

Lips skinned back from my teeth. I screamed, a short hawk-cry of frustration, and spun, *dotani* blurring in a solid arc of silver, striking down an invisible foe, the knife flickering as I shouldered past another, and I was in an alley in Antai again, a brat of a merchant's son screaming he had *paid* for me, and he would *have* me, and his hired blades sought to trap me. Sick with the *jai* fever I'd been that winter, my body burning and shaking.

So many battles, each one trapped in bone and muscle, pain-path and sinew. When I stepped onto the Long Road to the Moon Herself, would I carry them with me?

I am no adai.

The thought, as usual, filled me an unsteady, clear red liquid, too bitter to be even gall-wine. I spun and slashed in tightening circles now, a pack of baying, invisible hounds taking solid form from memory's invisibility. Those lean shaggy creatures hunt the outskirts of Pesh, sacred to their fire-god's lamed son. One alone you may kill with impunity, but a group is the god's hunters, any caught drawing against them risking being stoned to death by an angry crowd. So they have grown wise and travel in packs, bold among the refuse and stone and clattering slave-chains.

What I had been seeking came to me, quiet as a thief, all a-sudden as an assassin's strike.

For a single blessed moment, everything fell away. Cold, hunger, exhaustion, the tangle of honor and responsibility and need. No-space flowered inside me, the peace that comes when the battle reaches white heat and you are no longer a collection of muscles and pain-paths but something else, where every enemy is invisible because you are dancing, *dancing*, only with yourself.

Dotani held high, knife braced and low, the *gla*-stance, used by the caged fighters in Hain when they have won a fight and one more link is struck from the debt holding them. If they die on the sands of the great arenas, impiety or shame does not attach to their families; all stain is considered expunged with blood.

What do you seek to wipe away, Kaia?

I no longer knew. Sides heaving, sweat freezing under my clothes and salt in my eyes stinging, I tipped my head back and cried out again, another hawk-scream. My arms dropped, and I realized a hush had fallen.

Some of the Skaialan had stopped to watch, axes or blades hefted to their shoulders. My *dotani* blurred back into its sheath; I turned away from their pale, hungry gazes and found my cloak in the hands of my *s'tarei*, standing beside the rack of maces, his own cheeks and nose red with cold.

MANY A SONG

THE SKAUNA deep in the bowls of Kalburn's keep was not a bath but the heat was welcome, and so were dry clothes. D'ri said nothing beyond commonplaces; nor did I. Breakfast was in the same hall as last night, a quieter affair than the great evening meal. Redfist was up to both elbows in a gigantic platter of heavily spiced chopped-fine meat trapped in thin intestinal casings, accompanied by boiled meatroot and their yeast-flower bread; my own porridge had enough sweet thick fruit syrup to rot the teeth of a Rijiin flower-seller, and the layer of condensed fat on top, I was told, was sweetened milk. No matter how unappetizing, the heaviness of the fats would fuel the warming breath, so I set to with a will, still occasionally shivering, and did not look at Emrath Needleslay, whose wide grey eyes were red-rimmed that morning. Whatever had passed between her and Redfist was private, certainly, but it hung between them even as they ate elbow-to-elbow.

"There is news," Darik said, finally, his own plate piled with the strange gut-meat. It smelled heavy, and oddly toothsome. "The red one was seeking you this morning, and thought you had left." His intonation was not quite that of a *s'tarei* to his *adai*, and it stung for a brief moment.

He had cause, and yet. The fire in the greatest hearth of the hall was a low, slumbrous beast; those who clustered the long tables could see their breath. Some great houses in the North heat their innards with the deep fire of tortured earth, Kalburn was hollowed out before such an art had reached its full stature and its harnessing of such heat is uncertain in the higher floors. They saw it as a mark of pride, those who sheltered in the stone cube, and hardiness.

"And you did not?" I used the form of the question that expressed arch disbelief; speaking G'mai to him was no less a thorny pleasure than it had always been. I longed for fish, for piri-sauce, for flatbread. Proper food, *real* food.

"Unless you were leaving to find this Dunkast and slit his throat, I did not think it likely." Among the mellifluous G'mai words, the Skaialan's name was an outcropping of sterile, ugly rock.

"Now *there* is an idea." I poked my wooden spoon at the porridge. "Do you think I should?" An attempt at bleak sellsword humor.

Ammerdahl Rikyat would have understood, and laughed, a sharp chuckle.

Darik did not look at me, choosing instead to gaze out onto the babble of breakfast and the fire in its wide, low home. "Would you care if I did not?" His inflection was sharply formal, a parent taking a child to task.

I pushed my chair back, swept my bowl and spoon up, and skirted the back of his chair. Stamping down the dais-steps was easy, but the problem of where to sit was not quite as simple. I settled for a half-empty table far from the great hearth, in a particularly dank corner, and did not look at the dais.

Childish? Perhaps. Yet if even he would treat me as something to be herded or chided, it was the only response I could give without reaching for a blade.

I have swallowed worse than that bowl of porridge, but precious little has threatened to choke me as much.

"Wellnow. What do I see?" A broad, burring stream of tradetongue and Skaialan, low and pleasant, along the rhythm of a Skaialan accent like a *torkascruagh*'s plodding gait. "A *walkir*, come to eat with the *tain*." A platter loaded with the spiced casing-meat, meatroot, and their strange bread banged upon the table, and the black-bearded fellow I had noticed last night lowered himself cautiously onto the bench on the other side. He also had an extra mug of sofin, and slid it across the wooden expanse until it halted next to my bowl.

I studied him while I cleaned my spoon of fruit syrup. "He calls me that too." I tilted my head at the dais, indicating Redfist, who appeared not to have noticed my arrival *or* departure. "Is it a compliment?" My Skaialan was careful, but correct enough.

Or the new arrival pretended it was. "Oh, aye." Fine teeth peeped cheerfully from the dark brush covering the lower half of his face. His nose was straight and proud, perhaps never broken. "We do not see the Blest People much in the Highlands, but we have tales. Ye be Gemerh, then?"

No. There was no denying it. "Yes." *A flawed child, and a flawed adai.* Though that would mean nothing to him.

"And you have traveled this far to help Rainak Redfist retake his clan-seat?" Those dark, thoughtful eyes were well on their way to swallowing me whole.

"We met over-the-sea." I watched him in return.

He did not let it halt his absorption of breakfast.

"It must be quite a tale." His brooch, the crescent with the pin through it, marked him as one of Emrath's guard. The *tain*, a lord's retainers. Later, I learned that a woman has no *tain* unless she is the last of her chieftain-family, or she is the Lady of Kalburn.

If I was alone among my kind, Emrath Needleslay was likewise among her own. I did not know, then, if she counted it a curse.

"Perhaps Redfist will tell it to you, my lord…?" I let the end of the sentence trail upwards, question clearly audible. It is not inflected as Hain, the language of giants, but around the Rim and everywhere else I have traveled, a question is spoken uphill.

"Jorak Blacknose, at your service, *walkir.*" Hunching his shoulders gave the impression of a bowing *torkascruagh*; his smile widened and was, for a giant barbarian, charming. His eyebrows met over his nose, a shelf of vigorous black bramble. "You are Kaia Steelflower." He handled the foreign slurry of tradetongue passable well. "And it is a pleasure to exchange names with ye."

I changed to tradetongue too. "May the Sun shine upon you." It was a Shainakh greeting, but an appropriate wish for this hideous place. The entire stone pile reeked of their strange spices, their heavy fur, and the oil they used to lift dirt away. Would the smell wash out when I returned to Antai?

If I returned to civilization again, I would need many, many baths.

My new eating companion used a spear-spoon to bring slices of gutmeat to his mobile mouth. "Did your…companions tell ye of the news?"

"Not yet. I have had a busy morn." *And a sleepless night.*

"Ah." Bright interest, reined but sharp, filled his dark gaze. It was a relief to find one among the giants who was not bleached by the cold. "Well, the Feru-laine—ye know who he is?"

His eyebrows, I finally realized, reminded me of the caterpillars the Hain use to make a raw cloth, soft, strong, and highly prized. The Skaialan hold all their body hair in high esteem, unlike the Rijiin and their perpetual shaving.

It either irritated or pleased me that he did not take my knowledge of the Ferulaine for granted. I could not decide which. "I am told he wishes to kill Redfist. And that the *thing* last night was of his making." My feet barely touched the floor if I stretched my boot-toes. Would I eventually have the urge to swing them, like a child at a feast? I hoped not.

"Oh, aye." Jorak Blacknose nodded. "Then ye have been told aright, lady Iron-Bloom. Tis said he has been seen on the Highroad, approaching Kalburn."

Emrath said as much. Good. Then Redfist may kill him and I shall return to Antai. The thought was powerfully attractive. "Is that so?"

"Tis said, but the truth of it, who knows?" A wide, startlingly liquid shrug, heavy shoulders lifting, dropping. He wore the Needleslay's clan-colors, but there was a broad bar of yellow stripe up one edge of his *kelta*—for so they call the huge rectangle of fabric that makes their skirts and wraps about their upper bodies. "If yon Conniaght Crae wishes to lead, there is much to be done."

"And your interest in those deeds would be?" In other words, *show me your dice, barbarian, and I shall consider showing you mine.*

"I am a bard, lady Kaia." Again, that smile, and those flashing dark eyes. He was dangerous, this one, using honey where a knife would not do. The quick intelligence in his gaze would whet more than one edge, and those he turned against would not feel the blade until he twisted it. "Many a song shall be sung of this, no matter how it ends. I intend to make certain of as much."

Another lutebanger. For a moment, I almost wish we had carried Gavrin along. To hear him put this Skaialan giant in his place with a song or two might have been satisfying, had I any illusions that he could do so. "That is very well," I said. "You may also do me a favor."

"Ah, now there is a request from a lady, and one I cannot refuse."

I found the attempt at flattery as bleakly amusing as any other I have been subjected to. "Good. Leave me out of the songs, Blacknose." What a *name*. "I had a lutebanger trailing me before we came North, and have only just managed to shake him from my keel."

With that, I bent myself to my porridge, and the Skaialan, perhaps wisely, said nothing more. He ate steadily, and he did not stare at me.

Darik, at the high table, did.

RISK WHEREVER WE LAND

Kalburn Keep's battlements were well-crafted, and if not for the wind cutting through every layer of cloth or fur in its way, they might even have been pleasant to stroll upon. My first compass of their rectangle course I spent looking outward, over the city and distant shatter-mountains, imagining an army determined to crack this stone nut. How would they approach? Of course, the outer city and the tentacles along the trade-roads would be put to the torch, the stone buildings blackened, timbered roofs and internal walls probably well-seasoned and capable of great blazing. The slum-quarters held a great deal more stone than, say, Antai, for earth-bones were probably cheaper to build with, here. The great forests meant wood was not virtually unknown, though, as it is on the Danhai plains or in the great bowl of the desert Pesh lays claim to. Trade routes over that baking expanse follow hidden watercourses, the lands beyond full of fable and strangeness.

One day, I had thought to wander that far. There had always seemed time enough later. I could have used a measure of that baking heat now.

My second circling of the battlements was much slower, my gaze directed over the shorter inner wall. I studied the hills and valleys of the keep's roofs, occasionally peering over the edge to check the map I was building inside my skull. I am not overly troubled by heights, but looking down that dizzying drop into a bailey or collection of other buildings clustering the rock-chunk like chicks under a hen was faintly uncomfortable. In a ship's rigging, at least you have a chance of landing in the sea.

Falling onto stone is a different proposition indeed.

To siege this place would be a drawn-out affair; the keep had two wells driven deep enough that the water was drawn unfrozen, the skaunas and the deep fires of earth to provide at least some measure of heat, and the only trouble would be the defenders running out of firewood and resorting to furniture— the cold would be worse outside the keep, and even worse in the wasteland outside the old city walls once the siege-burning was done. Great vaults were tunneled into the roots of the keep-rock for beast and human fodder alike; a few could hold here against many.

If they had to.

I had almost finished my second survey when Darik found me. My hood pulled close, I was a statue gaze-mapping routes over the rooftop's pitches and noting each place that looked slick or tenuous. The great expanses of slate tile were full of hidden dells, and there would be small life clinging in protected places. Moss and its cousins, maybe more, ready to turn a foot or cause a slide. It would take time to learn that terrain, and the map seen from above sometimes bore little relation to the difficulty of actual traversing. Once I had the Keep's roofs inside my head, I could turn my attention to the city's.

Darik's arrival changed the tenor of the wind's cry, a *s'tarei's* fierce silence blunting all else. He settled against the inner wall, his face turned to the opposite side of the archer's path. Looking outward, as I gazed in. We stood like that for some while, my hands turned to knots under my cloak and the warming breath melting through me, a stove in my belly and twin flares upon my cheeks. Banners, as the Hain rise when they march to war.

Finally, I took a step, but not away. No, I moved toward him, and our shoulders, both padded with heat-conserving layers, touched. "I dislike this place," I said, finally, softly. If he chose to, he could take it as the salute before a duel, or he could treat it as a bare statement of fact.

I did not know which direction he would turn, and hoped it was not the former.

"As do I." Equally quiet, and his weight shifted a fraction, just enough to lean into mine. Was it forgiveness, or did he crave the contact? I could not decide which it was for me, either.

Eye-walking the rooftop roads meant I did not have to look at him. Yet I did, studying his wind-mussed hair, the tips of his ears poking through dark silk, his eyes half-closed against the wind's stinging.

Finally, I spoke again. "We cannot leave him to face this alone." Again, the words could open a duel, or end one. Did he notice the *we*, instead of *I*? Did it please him?

It was not a *submission*, I told myself. It was a mark of respect for a *s'tarei* too fine for me.

He was still, a rock facing the keening wind. "I am unwilling to risk my *adai*."

"It is no risk." It was not quite a lie, but I still felt

the inward pinch of conscience. "Or very little of one. Misfortune strides through every part of the world, D'ri. There is danger wherever we may land."

"True." He exhaled sharply, his hair stripped from his face, blue-black strands lifting and dancing. His *dotanii* hilts, riding his shoulders, glittered sharply in the grey light. More sleet was coming, the wind carried water in its mineral breath. "If we face another of those unclean things, you *must* not seek to strike it. They are dangerous to *adai*."

If he would not duel, perhaps we could discuss this calmly. "Even one with little Power?" I shifted further, leaning into him. "Possessing her own *dotani*, and well acquainted with its use?"

His answering pressure was a balm, tension draining from his frame. "Any *adai*, Kaialitaa." *Small sharp thing*, a play on my name. "Were I the *s'tarei* I should be, I would take you from here, whether you willed or no."

"Were you ruthless enough to strike me unconscious, you might succeed." The cut escaped before I could halt it. My breath plumed before the wind snatched the words free. "I will not be dragged, D'ri. I have charted my own course for years, and I do not leave my friends to suffer alone."

At least he did not take much offense. "Not until they betray you." He moved, a half-turn, and was behind me, his hands at my waist. The wind pushed his back, and the sudden cessation of its bite against my shoulders was welcome. "Is that what will loosen your stubbornness?"

That, or damage to you. Did he hear the thought? The *taih'adai* was a painful weight between us, space he was perhaps learning to leave me. Once he managed that skill, I could let him approach. "I do not think Redfist would betray me."

"You did not think your friend Rikyat would, either."

I winced, and shifted to tradetongue, an old proverb from the Freetowns. "I am sure of nothing, save steel."

"Then I am as steel, for you." He rested his chin atop my head, and his intonation was intimate again, *s'tarei* to *adai*. He did not play upon the word for sword, merely chose the term for a large chunk of ore that threatens to break the smith's hammer. "And I will not ask you to turn aside."

A tightness I had not known I carried loosened a fraction inside my chest, then a fraction more. "I am sorry." Perhaps he would not hear me, over the wind. "I do not mean to wound you."

"Likewise." His hands tightened, arms sliding around me as far as he could reach over the bulk of borrowed skins. "If I were ruthless enough to drag you, Kaia, would you forgive me?"

"I do not know," I replied, and there the matter lay. Perhaps it was wisdom that he did not ask further, and perhaps it was mercy that I did not offer more explanation. Eventually, it was too cold to remain still even with the warming breath, and when I moved to finish my second circuit of the walls, he followed.

I CAN BE NO LESS

THE HIGHLAND'S VALLEY-PLAINS, in winter, bear some resemblance to a great desert. Their great forests, smothered under snow, nevertheless bear life in their depths, and trade from their fringes supports the plainsdwellers. In summer, the crops from the flatter land and terraced hills spread into the forests, and thus it has been since Redfist's kind moved into those lands.

The Standing Stones, the jewel in the richest navel of farmland that rests under snow and ice during the brutal winters, are held to predate Ska-ialan arrival. There are five, rough, milky, rose-shot pillars, spirals etched into their surfaces by some craft now lost to time or murder. The stone floor they stand sentinel over is also not native to these parts, a slab of gray flecked like a speckled egg, polished smooth. In the middle of this rises a blackened stone weeping reddish traces—skymetal, driven deep into the earth, its edges meeting the speckle-stone seamlessly. I would have suspected the Pensari had spread this far, given the cream-skin of the giants and the paleness of the five pillars, but the Standing

Stones do not exhale the chill retained by everything those white worshippers of cold death touched.

The top of the skymetal chunk is flattened, and chained to its bulk with heavy, flat, spiral-carved links is the hammer, its massive head chased with running, knotted runes. The Skaialan say it is not Kroth's, but his father Gurath's, that giant god who ate most of his progeny before his son returned from hanging on a massive tree at the world's core, bleeding and furious, and crushed his father's godly skull.

It sounds bizarre, but no less so than any other god-story. Nothing that went into Gurath's stomach ever returned, but stray creeping fleas who had hidden among his ear and nose hairs are held to be the first humans.

The hammer is of stone, with its highly chased skymetal head. It is *exceeding* large, its haft requiring a double-grip from even the most massive of Redfist's countrymen. Only those with the permission of the Lady of Kalburn may lift it, and even if one is permitted he may be struck down if any of their gods, much less Kroth their chieftain, does not agree that the wielder is fit for it. Dunkast of the Ferulaine was indeed approaching along the snowy roads to attempt the feat, but it was Rainak Redfist who accompanied the Keeper of the Stones, her golden hair wound with blue and green ribbons, to the stone floor and the milk-colored pillars that afternoon.

I shivered my way along, a few steps behind Redfist, Darik to my left. The crowd, red-nosed, bright-eyed, and braving a freshening wind and an iron-grey sky pregnant with still-threatening sleet, lined the streets, oddly subdued. We walked from Kalburn's keep's eastern gate to the wall of the Old City and through the Needle Gate, then down a long slope of stone-paved road twitching back and forth to take advantage of hummocks swept clean by the north gale's howling. They are cunning in how they lay their roads, the Skaialan, and if the path under your feet takes a sudden turn, tis best to follow it rather than seeking a shortcut. *The more hurry, the less speed*, they say, and plenty of the wise in other countries agree.

It was a long journey, and a miserable one despite the warming breath and the bundle of furs I huddled in. Porridge was not enough to keep me warm through this, but the alternative was the heavy-spiced casing-meat. It did not seem *clean* to eat something carried about in guts, even if the bowels are washed and soaked and washed again. I concentrated on Redfist's broad back, moving at a steady clip. His *kelta* was his clan's colors; apparently Emrath had either kept the length of cloth hidden since before her marriage of convenience...or she had produced it in secret afterward.

Which gave me much food for thought.

D'ri was quiet, the fierce silence of a *s'tarei*, and his uneasy awareness of the crowd in our wake matched my own. Once his left boot slipped upon a rimed cobble, and my hand shot out, closing about his wrist. Unnecessary, since he had not lost his balance, and he did not pull away. Instead, he turned his hand, mine slid down, and our half-gloved fingers meshed. If he had to draw, it would be his left-hand blade, but he did not let go.

Nor did I. For the first time, we walked linked, the motif repeated over and over in G'mai art. Sculpture, painting, tapestry all have their conventions, and the twinning echoes through them all.

The warming breath became easier, and my shivers eased. Perhaps his did, as well. Well past noon, we reached the Standing Stones, cupped in their dell that nonetheless does not hold the snows or a great deal of ice. Somehow, falling water of any kind avoids the five-cornered cup, and the closer we drew to it, the more uncomfortable I became. A pressure along the throat, bulging behind my eyes, a half-heard snatch of melody forcing the ears to strain.

Power. Here, in this cold, benighted place. My hand tightened in Darik's, and he glanced at me, dark eyes fathomless.

Emrath Needleslay, wrapped in an ell of blue-green, striped, and cross-hatched cloth, halted at the edge of the speckled floor. The tallest Stone, towering at her left, held a faint reflection of her bright hair, a ghost in its carved depths. A rusting staple driven deep into the side of the strange rock and a similarly rusting ring depended from it, creaking slightly as the wind pushed with greedy invisible fingers.

The crowd crunched through ice-crust and and hardened mud to spread out, children bundled to roundness, men and women in blue-and-green or dun cloth, pale uncooked-dough cheeks and bushy beards running from gold to ruddiness, with a sprinkling of dark heads here and there. Emrath's *tain* had not followed her closely, mixing with the onlookers instead; later, I learned that the Lady of Kalburn walks alone to the Stones, and while she is upon the path, to strike or offer insult to her is a crime against Kroth himself.

Redfist glanced at Emrath. Her cheeks were vivid with the cold, her head lifted proudly. The crowd became a mouth, spreading around a piece of solidified sugar slightly too large for it. They jostled, the few who accidentally stepped onto the speckle-stone pulled back by their fellows and chided in whispers.

"Are ye certain, Emrath?" Redfist sounded...tentative? For perhaps the first time since I had picked his pocket, he did seem somewhat uncertain.

It suited him. His calves, pale and furred with red glinting into gold, were also stipple-gemmed with melted ice.

Emrath Needleslay smiled rather bitterly. "I am the Keeper of the Stones." She stripped her thick knitted gloves away, her large, finely modeled fingers gleaming slightly with sweet oil. "If you are determined, Rainak, I can be no less."

Again, I almost liked her, despite her insults and her disdain. D'ri pulled on my hand; I stepped close to him. The prickling, buzzing discomfort intensified. It was the same sensation that kept me away from the witch outside Vulfentown, with her creaking, cawing birds and her slatternly, high-piled, grey-curled hair. She had Power, and plenty of it, and why she chose to live outside a Freetown and occasionally sell bits of dice-luck or darker things was no concern of mine. Witches did what they willed, or as they must, and we avoided each other. Or at least, we had all during my travels.

Now I was thinking I could have mastered my instinctive avoidance and learned a thing or two from one of that secretive sisterhood and their ways, hidden as the Moon's own. I had not, though, and this place called forth a deep welling of caution.

No doubt Janaire would have been fascinated, were she not safe in Antai. I shivered, and D'ri's arm slid over my shoulders. More welcome warmth, and I accepted it. An assassin here seemed...unlikely.

"Very well." Redfist's chin turned to his shoulder, and he regarded us sidelong with one blue, bloodshot eye. "K'ai, lass, whatever happens, do *not* enter the Stones."

"Fear not." The words sounded thin, and cold, and my teeth threatened to chatter them into bits. "I've no desire to."

It only occurred to me later that he did not similarly caution Darik.

The Needleslay shook her hands, much as a Rijiin acrobat will before performing. She reached, hesitated for a bare moment, and grasped the iron ring with both bare palms and curling her naked fingers through, despite the danger of freezing to the metal.

Her back stiffened and the prickles raced over me, painful now. My knees threatened to loosen, and when the Lady of Kalburn spoke again, her voice boomed from each of the five stones, echoes multiplying from the floor as well. *"Who are ye,"* she said, in heavy, rolling Skaialan far too deep for even her capacious chest to summon, *"to stand before the Stones?"*

Thin, unhealthy pink phosphorescence spread in tendrils from the iron staple, pale against the daylight. My mouth was dry as the Danhai plains in summerscorch. Darik's eyelids lowered a fraction, and the *taran'adai* between us tautened.

"I am he who calls the Clans." Redfist did not bellow, but the words were clear. They echoed strangely against the stone as well. "I am Connaight Crae, Rainak Redfist, son of Doural Redfist, and I hae the right and the will."

At first I thought Emrath was swelling, for she seemed to grow taller. Then the iron hoop clanked, rattling, and her skirts rustled strangely. Her body lifted, her boot-tips dropping as her toes pointed, and my breath caught. She *floated*, her toes barely brushing the ground. Her head tipped back, ribbon-wrapped braids slithering against each other. She said something in Skaialan, low and guttural, that I could not translate.

Redfist replied, and then, head high, he stepped onto the specklestone floor.

Whatever I expected, it was not the spreading of that diseased pinkish light, dripping down the largest stone and radiating below and between Emrath's boot-toes. The other stones bore rosettes of that strange light struggling against the health-giving glow of the great daylamp, and a crack-creaking ran under the five-sided cup as a massive sheet of ice will shift as the temperature changes.

Redfist leaned forward, his broad shoulders dropping. His clubbed hair blew back, his beard pushed by invisible fingers, and his new furred cloak—a gift, no doubt, from the Needleslay—flapped. It was *wrong*; cloth and hair moved *against* the wind seeking to sting water from my eyes and push me into Darik.

I have seen a great many uncanny things in my wanderings. Very little has raised the fear-flesh on me, having seen wonders enough in my homeland; Power moves as it wills and performs as it pleases. I had, however, never seen a giant struggle across a stone floor while something huge and almost-visible seeks to crush him, a flea between fingernails.

Words dropped from Emrath's slack mouth, resounding against the five pillars. Harsh, unlovely, and much deeper than her speaking-voice—I had seen this before, in the great city of Taryam-Arat, where their goddess speaks through the mouths of her followers, each a single syllable in her chorus. The Moon is jealous of her people, so a G'mai is not overly troubled by other gods, but still…what was it like, to have something fill you, speak through your mouth in such a fashion?

Once, the Moon spoke through a G'mai, and once only. That was Belariaa, who brought us the twinning and drove back the Great Dark.

I wondered if *she* had sounded like this.

Step by step, Redfist struggled across the wide floor as Emrath chanted. It was no great distance, but he looked...too small. My eyes ached, struggling with a view that made no *sense*, and Darik exhaled softly, his gaze sharpening too. The crowd stilled. Furious mutters raced through them—betting, no doubt, on how far he would reach. A certain number seemed to wish him to fail, and I longed to reach for my *dotani*.

Between one moment and the next, the tension snapped. Redfist almost staggered, reeling forward, and Emrath's chant halted.

A breathlessness descended. The wind fell into silence, a vast weight pressing down like a pregnant beast about to bear. Redfist lunged, and his red-furred hands closed about the hammer-haft. The altar-chunk of rust-bleeding skymetal it was attached to ran with that same weeping, pinkish light, and the stillness, unnatural as the rest of this rite, grew so vast even the crowd of giants and their pups held collective breath caged in their lungs.

Redfist screamed, a guttural cry of effort, and the hammer quaked. It groaned as he lifted it high overhead, its chain rattling and clashing like a live thing. Then he brought it down, onto the flattened top of the skymetal chunk.

BOOM.

D'ri told me afterward how the impact sent that reddish flame rocketing skyward, how Emrath sagged, thumping back to frozen earth and clinging to the iron ring to keep herself upright. Redfist dropped the massive hammer, and cried aloud again, a victory-bellow with an edge, full of the pride of a wounded animal that can nevertheless crush its tormenters before bled to death's cold embrace.

I did not see what happened next, for the freezing

and the alien Power conspired to drive me sideways into D'ri's shoulder, my head ringing fit to blind me. He all but dragged me back to the keep on the first wave of a crowd cheering our gingery barbarian, since, after all, Kroth had not struck him down.

Rainak Redfist had been judged worthy. And the clans, from one end of the Highlands to the other, had been summoned to assembly.

ARGUE WITH A DUEL

"My apologies." Darik held a wooden cup of near-boiling sofin to my lips, and I pushed his hand away to take it myself as I sagged upon a three-legged wooden stool. The Northern drink was not chai, but it was wonderfully warming nonetheless. "I shall be more careful of you, Kaia."

"No need to apologize. Every land has its witchery," I muttered. "I am simply unused to it striking me upon the head." It was worse than the aftermath of a tavern brawl, and I missed being largely unaffected by such things. Denial of my own Power, practiced since childhood, had inured me to much of the world's uncanny. Now, with a *s'tarei*, I was no longer as immune.

I could not decide if it was a comfort, or a worry. Or both, a twin-headed wyrm.

"No *adai* would be comfortable with such a thing," he agreed gravely. Beads of sleet, caught in his hair, glistened.

"Is she well?" Redfist's face rose over his shoulder, a rosy-scruffed moon with melted drops caught in his beard and hair. "Kaia?"

"Well enough." I took stock, barely remembering

being dragged inside Kalburn keep again. At least this room was familiar, the same one the Needleslay had insulted me in yesterday, with its half-finished tapestry and its half-wooden walls. Emrath had waved aside her female attendants and their chivvying with a single weary motion outside the door.

The grey-eyed Lady of Kalburn, transparently pale, slumped in a chair by the fireplace and sipped at her own cup of spiced wine. She studied Redfist's back, her expression somewhere between thoughtful and exhausted. Sleet-melt dropped from her skirt and overshoes, and when she caught my gaze her large bloodless mouth drew down, a slight grimace.

Was it envy, upon her face? I have seen such an expression before, but rarely upon a woman. Most of them, except for fellow sellswords, consider me an unlucky creature at best.

I decided whatever the Needleslay was contorting her face over was best left unaddressed. Instead, I turned to the truly pressing question. "What happens now?"

"I have been judged worthy by Kroth Himself." Redfist nodded, as if I'd posed a profound riddle. His blue eyes were bloodshot, and he moved as if his right arm pained him somewhat. He stretched his hands as sellswords often do, restoring flexibility to fingers frozen by practice, injury, or cold. "Next the Clans send their envoys. If all goes well, they will refuse to obey Dunkast any further, and—"

"And apples will fall from the sky, and the rivers will not freeze but run with wine." Emrath's laugh was a masterpiece of sharp bitterness. A tendril of golden hair had come loose of her braids and fell in her face. The dishevelment, slight as it was, suited her. "Or is it that ye've taken up lying now, Rainak?"

My head ached, a tender fruit balancing upon a

too-thin stem. "Well, Dunkast is on his way here. Perhaps you may simply kill him, and the problem solves itself." *And we may return to Antai as soon as the Pass melts.*

The prospect had much to recommend it. Sofin, too hot to truly drink, was nevertheless bracing, and I inhaled its scent gratefully.

"Oh, aye." Emrath lifted her heavy-carved wooden cup, a sarcastic toast. Her ear-drops glittered, lying against fair hair. "Were it that simple, my lady Elvish, it would have been done by others long since."

Mother Moon, I hate that word. "If you have nothing helpful to add, Needleslay, perhaps you should hold your tongue."

"Quarrelsome women." Redfist's teeth showed, a strained smile. He disdained a chair, and his hairy shins were stippled with road-spatter. "It gave me a turn to see ye struck, Kaia. Perhaps your Durran has the right of it."

"I begin to think you do not wish my company or my protection, Redfist." I took a gulp of sofin, scorching all the way down. "And I do not think this likely to be simple at all. That does not mean I cannot jest, or wish it were so. Of course, your enemy is on his way hither; he must sleep sometime, and I am hardly the worst when it comes to quiet knifework."

That made a stunned silence fill the room. A knot of sap-heavy wood piled in the fireplace instead of blackrock popped, and I did not flinch at the sound. Darik straightened, touched my shoulder with two fingers, and paced to the window.

A prince of the Dragon Throne might not like the idea of assassination, but any who have dabbled in politics understand its efficacy.

"So this is *your* Black Brother, Rainak?" Enrath

studied me. Her grey eyes were bloodshot too; it could not have been comfortable to bear the invisible force thundering through the Stones. Though I had considered myself the only flawed G'mai, we are still bred to Power. Not many others may say the same. "An elvish—"

My temper snapped. "Say that word again, Needleslay, and I will call you to the dueling ground." I tested my legs, found they were more than adequate, and stood, setting the cup down on a small table next to the wobbling stool. It was perhaps a child's seat, being my size rather than Redfist's, and I did not like to be perched upon it. My restlessness demanded motion; I longed to be moving.

"Will ye, now." She dropped her gaze into her own cup, though, and moved her feet slightly, kicking her skirts free of her overshoes. "A common bint challenging the Lady of Kalburn. The bards shall have a fine time with that."

"I've seen her duel, Emrath." Redfist sighed, gustily, and turned to rubbing at his right shoulder. "Ye'd be wise to keep thy mouth closed."

"Oh, so ye have what ye wish of me, and now it's *keep thy mouth closed, Emrath.*" She shook her head, her hair rasping against the high-carven seatback. The fire spoke again, popping counterpoint. "Fine manners thou did learn in the underlands, boyo."

"I might almost think she wishes that Dunkast man here to defend her," Darik commented from the window, softly, in G'mai. Afternoon light, failing swiftly, fell across his hair and the planes of his face, and I felt, again, the weary astonishment that so fine a princeling had left the Blessed Land, come over sea and hill, and decided to attach himself to *me*, of all people.

"I might, as well." It was good to find something to agree with my *s'tarei* about. Then I changed to tradetongue, but did not load it with Skaialan. Let her work to understand my speech, this woman. "This Ferulaine may well arrive before the clans do. What do you plan in *that* event, Redfist-my-friend?"

A curious look crossed Redfist's broad barbarian face, nose wrinkling slightly with perplexity. "Well."

I waited, setting my course for the window as well. Halfway there, the silence grew heavy, and I swung about. My boots, dripping, left marks on the scattered rushes. "You *do* have a plan, do you not?"

He spread his hands. Vivid red marks upon his palms showed the print of the hammer-haft. "I've called the Clans. Tis enough, for now."

Is it? I all but boggled at him, my jaw-hinge suspiciously loose. "You mean you have *no* plan? You have not thought upon—"

He scowled at me, returning to rubbing at his shoulder. It was a new thing; in the South, he had been, if not sunny, at least phlegmatic. "I have thoughts aplenty. There is much he must answer for, my brother."

Here was a new wrinkle to the fabric. *Bastard* could have been a use-term; I knew little of the High-lands kin-structure. "Brother? I thought you said he was a—"

"Aye, but he was like a brother to me." Redfist dropped his hands and turned his chin, looking to the stone mantel and the glow of burning wood. The chimney made a low sound as wind swept across its top, like a Rijiin side-flute. "Until he killed my father."

"You mentioned that." I cupped my earthenware mug, enjoying its short-lived heat. The sofin was

122

cooling quickly. Even inside, a Highlands winter seeks to eat what living fire it may find.

"That is not the tale I heard." Emrath stared at the fire, possibly deciding it was the safest quarter to rest her gaze upon. "Half my clan must be angry I walked a kinslayer to the Stones. The other half, well. Kroth has judged thee, how can *I* argue?"

I had little sympathy for the Needleslay's clan-troubles. "Precisely *how* did your father die, Redfist?"

"I cannae tell." It was hard to believe the ruddy giant could grow pale, but he did. "The morning of battle, he was stone-cold in his tent, and our clan surprised by the Ferulaine striking before dawn."

Interesting. "Poison?" Suddenly the sofin did not seem nearly as appetizing.

The corners of our barbarian's mouth turned down, his mouth pursing, hiding in his beard. Drying, it sprang up in a tangle. "I am no assassin, to know such things."

"*I* am." I arrived at Darik's shoulder, gazed out into a darkening afternoon. The sky held a promise of snow instead of sleet, its infinite depths lightening slightly as the wind chilled just a fraction. Just enough. "You may tell much from the way a man chooses to kill." It was an old Hain proverb. "And when you know a man, you know how to kill him." *That* was a Clau saying, and I longed suddenly, fiercely, to see Kesamine at the Swallows Moon again. At least *there* I could eat proper food, and take a real bath.

Silence, again, filled the room to the brim.

"When he arrives…" The words were quiet, and level, without any of Redfist's usual bluff, hearty noise. If he spoke thus more often, I might well have to revise my opinion of his temper, not to mention his dangerousness. "When he does, I shall challenge him to trial, and we shall see."

"Rainak..." Emrath lowered her goblet with a troubled frown.

I could hardly argue with a duel, having fought my fair share. "It might be best to simply let me sink a knife into his liver," I pointed out. "And if he has witchery upon him—"

"Kaia." Darik shook his head. "*I* shall kill him, should it come to that. The foul gloves are dangerous to an *adai*, and the Power of this country—"

"I am the better assassin, D'ri." *You are far too fine for such things.* My shoulder touched his again, and I stared across sloping, slate-tiled roofs, up at the deepening bruise of the sky.

"*Neither* of ye will kill him." A hard smacking sound—a ham-sized fist, driven into the opposite palm. If Redfist winced at the impact against his bruised hands, I could not tell. "I shall be meeting him in trial, and let Kroth decide. And if by some foul witchery he strikes me down, Emrath will smuggle ye twain south as she did me."

"I will?" Emrath laughed. It might have been a pleasant sound, but for its lack of true amusement. "Oh, aye, I will, if only to be free of them. Ye are just as ye were, Rainak Redfist."

"The underlands could nae change me, *corra-luagnh*."

"No." She rose, setting her goblet down upon a small ebonwood table with a slight, distinct noise. "I suppose they could not. Nothing will."

Skirts moved, a low subtle music. When she closed the heavy wooden door, it was softly, as if upon an invalid's room.

I leaned further into Darik. His answering pressure was a balm, and outside the glass, frostflowers etched in its corners, fresh, fattening flakes of snow began to fall. They would melt at first, dying against damp street and wet roof, but the sacrifice of the first ranks laid ground for the next, waves upon waves of an inexhaustible army.

MEANT TO BE WHOLE

Some of the barbarians go direct from the *skauna* to the snows outside, casting themselves naked into drifts. The giants of the highlands hold that such a practice is healthful, and if they live near a stream or lake they will even chop holes in the ice and dip themselves after a long soak in the dry heat.

As far as I may tell, it explains Redfist's people— and their ways—*perfectly*.

The storm squatted over Kalburn, an iron-colored sky lowering to touch the rooftops and gouts of snow whirling on a cold, flirting wind. The battlements were a misery, the training-grounds even worse. I might have gone what the Shainakh call "wall-mad" if not for the *asal*—a long, timber-roofed courtyard running alongside a pillared gallery, used for weapons practice for the young, the recovering, or in weather too ill for even the *tain* to play at war's many games. A Skaialan boy is given a small blunted axe on his fifth name-day and taught its use. They may be suited for broadsword, mace, or the smaller dual axes, but their first weapon is always the *labirin*, also named the *tuag*. They do not prize flexibility or speed. A Skaialan brawler is a creature of raw power, and the quick or the versatile are seen as somewhat cowardly.

The *tain* practiced in the snow, their furred boots gripping with more surety than I would have believed possible, bodies steaming as they warmed and shrugged free of layers. I decided it was useless to do so unless I wished to freeze solid, and used the *asal* with D'ri. We followed each other through the forms. In my case, I adapted with a long knife reversed along my forearm, since I use but a single *dotani*. His twin blades, heavier, blurred through the movements with graceful precision, breath expelled in a small huff at the strike-moment. Their meat-pastes sat uneasy in my stomach, but once I took to eating I found they did keep me warmer.

Unsanitary or not, they fueled the warming breath wonderfully.

Darik matched his rhythm to mine, and we played the game—a little faster, a little slower, subtle clues from breath, the singing of cloven air, and the silence of the *taran'adai* calling the measures of the dance as Rijiin acrobats thump time with short sticks during their practices. I had an advantage; with concentration, I could *feel* his muscles begin the work of another move, and it was little trouble to follow. Sidestep, flowing through the second form, into the third, blending the two for a quarter-candlemark, then a shift to the other side and I took the lead, beginning the first cycle afresh. The first cycle is the mother of all; its simplicity is deceptive. You may spend a lifetime practicing its cadence and be well-prepared for any combat, yet have only scratched the surface of its applications.

Sweat, stinging my eyes. No, not mine, D'ri's. A cramp in his left calf, overridden with an application of will, my own leg threatening to seize up. I exhaled and he took the lead, swinging us both into the third form. Strike, release, catching your opponent's blade, turning his force back upon him. Stone underfoot, wood and stone above, the storm outside.

The Skaialan tie ropes from one post at a building's door to the neighbor's during what they call the White Howl, so they do not become lost in the disorienting whirl of snow and ice. I had thought this overly cautious until I saw my first Howl. There may be hells of blackness as the Pesh describe, or of fire as the Clau say, or even of yellow-painted chains and lamentation as most of the Hain—those masters of creating layers upon layers of hierarchy for their gods and spirits to wander—fear, but the one *I* think most likely is pure blowing white, and it is indistinguishable from the Highlands.

The space inside the *asal* changed, its emptiness shifting as yet another breathing creature disturbed its solitude. D'ri turned, so I did too, and we both watched Redfist halt several paces away, his hairy bare calves steaming and his big raw hands hanging at his sides. His furred face held a strange expression, one I have seen on too many outside the borders of the Blessed Land.

Wonder. Incomprehension. It was only a half-step from there to fear, and plenty chose to take it, continuing into the dull, righteous fury of someone who sees an offense to their gods and can only right it with blood. Perhaps here, among his countrymen instead of among the smaller brown people of the Rim, my strangeness was magnified for him.

"News?" D'ri lowered his *dotanii*, and I did the same, his motion pulling my own arms and legs along. I had to exhale sharply to free myself of the sensation, shaking my head as a nervous horse will fling rain from its mane.

"Aye." But Redfist's expression did not change. "How do ye move like that?"

"Training." Darik glanced at me. "And tis easier, when you can feel the movement in your own limbs."

"Ah." Redfist thrust his thumbs into his belt. "She feels yer pain."

"Do not ask *him* what I feel." I flicked my *dotani*, cleaning it of invisible blood of the other matter of murder, and it blurred back into its sheath. "What news then, my ruddy friend?"

"Dunkast has sent a message."

"What kind?"

"Sealed on parchment. I came to ask ye, K'ai, if ye would examine it for witchery."

My throat turned dry. It was a reasonable request to make of an *adai*, even one who had very little Power. Darik's own blades blurred home; he rolled his shoulders once, twice, dispelling stiffness. Warmed and loosened, we were now ready to face whatever battle loomed.

"I am not certain how much good my examination may do." I forced myself not to move my own shoulders. How far would I sink into D'ri? The more intimate aspects of the twinbond are not much spoken of to children; I left G'maihallan so young I did not know how far I would lose...myself. Or the self I *had* been.

We are meant to be whole, *adai* and *s'tarei*. What was I truly feeling, now that I no longer walked alone out of all my kin?

"But I shall do what I can." I bounced on my toes once, thrice, shook out my hands, finally convinced my body it was separate and I was its sole sovereign once more. Darik did not comment, and the *taran'adai* did not tell me what he felt.

Or was it that I chose not to look, to see?

∾

THE GREAT HALL was full of Emrath's *tain*, but they did not press close to the table where the item lay. The fire, mixed blackrock and timer, in the massive hearth was merely embers; she had been hearing petitioners today, and settling disputes. Emrath herself, the Lady of Kalburn, sat motionless upon the great bench chipped from the Keep's stone upon a dais carved from the same, her pale chin resting upon her hand. This was not the dining hall; this space in the heart of the keep was where she heard clan business and made judgments, the floor patterned with stone-dye they have since lost the craft of as well. They call it the First-Carved, and though it may not be strictly the first chamber bored into the giant chunk of stone, it certainly feels older than the rest. Only the *skauna* and storerooms were below, the earth-heat takes some little of the chill away, and the insulation of frozen earth and layers of stone blunted the edge of the Howl.

In such a hall, one feels the weight of stone overhead. I have not the fear-of-close-spaces, and yet it is...unpleasant, to breathe in such a place.

On a low table set to the left, meant to hold evidence in a dispute or tribute during a gifting session, lay the letter.

There was no glow of Power on the rectangular package with its strange spidery lettering. Highland text is not the picture-speaking, like Hain's, or the long curves, dots, and dashes of Shainakh, or even the mellifluous writing of my own country, words joined as twins, triplets, each phrase a single stroke halted only by the curve of a breaking-mountain rune. Each sound in Skaialan's consonant-heavy flow has its own angular symbol, and they string together word and phrase in reverse as lutebangers and other bards all over the Rim trap their music on paper: left to right, sounding out each symbol and holding it for the required duration. Strange, but there are as many different ways to write as there are hands to hold a brush or quill.

It is the leisure to learn such things that is spread unevenly over the world's surface.

In any case, I eyed the waterproofed parchment packet, seeking to look not merely with my eyes. With Janaire's careful lessons and the starmetal spheres, I even stood a chance of finding something amiss. "How was this delivered?"

"By a man in Ferulaine colors. Handed it to the door-guard, and vanished into the White Howl." Redfist shook his head. "The door-guard says he did not speak."

"Your Dunkast's eyes and hands are in this city, then." I folded my arms. My back itched with dried, flaking sweat under layers of clothing. I began to see the wisdom of their lacking baths; if I washed my hair it might well freeze solid. "I wonder..." There were bound to be some who favored Dunkast even among Emrath's *tain*, and my gaze drifted away from the packet to the group of Skaialan warriors on the other side of the hall in Emrath's colors, arranged by rows according to their rank, straining to hear what passed between us. More of them patrolled the Old City and the halls of the Keep, or carried her business with other chieftains along the snow-choked roads.

Which among them was avoiding this meeting for a dark reason, or had taken pains to attend for the same? I did not know nearly enough, though my observation of each one who passed me in the halls or attended the great daily dinner was habitual and exact, by now.

Redfist had no patience for my wondering. "Is there witchery upon it?"

He had taken to barking at me of late, and I had taken to slowing my replies, pausing before each and stringing the words together with much space between them. "None that *I* can tell, friend Redfist. Darik? Do you sense aught amiss?"

When my *s'tarei* spoke, it was in quiet, rolling G'-mai. "You would know before I would, *adai'mi*." All the same, he stood closer to me than usual, and on my right side, too, blocking my *dotani*-draw. He changed to tradetongue, pitching the words loudly enough to carry somewhat. "It seems to be merely a letter. Perhaps he wishes you a merry name-day."

A ripple of laughter, thin and nervous, passed through the assembly. Emrath's expression did not change. She simply watched, her large furred boots placed delicately, her ankles crossed. Her skirts arranged prettily and her great fur over-mantle pulled close, she did not seem to feel the cold. Perhaps she did not, bred to it as she was.

Redfist turned the packet over. The seal was a blot of black brittle wax with a strange snarling thing pressed into it—a wolf's head, in the Northern style. The same sigil was pressed upon coins from Ferulaine's mines and mints, and had no doubt decorated the pieces Corran Ninefingers had brought to Antai.

When Redfist broke the seal with a faint noxious *crack*, I tensed. But it was nothing, merely that wax behaves strangely when it has been frozen. The giant spread out the folded rag-made sheet inside. "Huh." He offered it to me.

I shook my head, disdaining to touch it. Whether it was prudence or cold fingers I did not care to decide. "I cannot read your writing well, yet. What does it say?"

"Very simple. He calls me *brother-that-was*. And tells me to go back to the outerlands, and I—and my elvish companions—may leave with our lives."

Of course this Dunkast would use that hateful word. News had reached him quickly of Redfist's companions, then. There were definitely spies among Emrath's *tain*.

A bitter clot of a laugh caught in my throat, squeezed its way out. "How generous."

"Not known for his generosity." It was Blacknose, who stepped from the ranks of the *tain* to address his lady's dais. His bare shins were not as hairy as his fellows'. Perhaps that was why his boots were higher, and fur-lined. "He fears you, Rainak Redfist."

"And well he should." Redfist eyed him. "Who be ye?"

"Jorak Blacknose." Proudly, head held high. "Bard to the Lady of Kalburn, and bearer of a willow wand."

"I've heard of ye." Redfist nodded. "Ye sang the Bull Lay entire on one drink of mead, did ye not?"

Blacknose swept a bow, rough but with some fillip of polish at the end. "I was young then, and reckless."

More amusement went through the assembled *tain*. It appeared the black-bearded one had some little fame. I turned my head, slightly; D'ri was watching Blacknose and Redfist with a sober, thoughtful expression. Whatever he was thinking, the *taran-adai* was silent.

Perhaps he did not wish me to know, or perhaps he was merely watchful.

Redfist turned back to me, and when he spoke, it was for the benefit of onlookers, a little too loudly and with more Skaialan than travel-pidgin. "What think ye, Kaia? Shall we hie back through the Pass and leave this fellow to do as he pleases?"

Ah, so now he was playing to the assembly, as those aim to who rule must often do. Wonders never ceased. "You think it likely he will keep his word? And there is the little matter of him murdering your father, and laying the deed at *your* door."

That sparked a shocked silence. Several of the *tain* glanced uncomfortably at each other, and I wondered how many of them had passed the kinslaying story along or half-believed it. It is a great sin among most, if not all, the world's peoples, to drive a blade into the heart of your own. Especially those who birthed you.

There are exceptions, of course. In Pesh girl-children can be slaughtered almost at will before their name-day, and the throne of any land is soaked with fratricide, patricide, and the like.

Except G'maihallan. And yet, the thick band of scarring on Darik's throat spoke of an act almost too blasphemous to be contemplated. To kill a *s'tarei* is to kill an *adai*, and that is the only thing the Moon will not forgive one of the Blessed.

"Aye," Redfist said, finally. There was a gleam to his blue eyes I had not seen before, and I suspected him of finger-combing his beard to make it tangle even more fiercely to match that of his countrymen. "There is that." He rolled the missive into his broad fist, and strode to the fireplace. "Does anyone else wish to read this?"

The paper of pounded rag and treefiber was passed from hand to hand among the *tain*. Finally, it was handed up to Emrath Needleslay on her stone bench. There was no cushion on the seat; perhaps she was bred be inured to such discomfort. It occurred to me that the weight of ceremony and obligation upon her was probably akin to the heavy expectations upon G'mai *adai*, and I did not care to feel any kinship with her, however small.

And yet...I did, in that moment.

She glanced over the letter's contents, and her expression did not change. She merely crumpled it into a wad, and tossed it back to Redfist, who caught the missile with surprising deftness.

The *tain*, to a man, tensed at their lady's movement, but they did not move. That small detail told me a great deal. So she was truly their leader, after all, and not merely a figurehead.

Interesting indeed. And when Redfist tossed the letter into the fireplace, many of the *tain* did not look away until they were certain the ink, the paper, and the wax-blot seal had burned.

ARRIVALS

WHEN THE HOWL FADED, Kalburn lay under an insulating, pale pall. I woke on a whiteglare morn two days after Dunkast's unwitched missive warm for the first time in a moonturn or three.

Still half-trapped in sleep's veils, I thought the ice, the barbaric giants, and all their ilk merely a dream, for a familiar weight lay upon on one side of me, D'ri's arm over my waist and his face in my hair. On my other side, a creature a little too tall to be a Vulfentown wharf-rat nestled, his own black hair stiff with unwashed oil and his chin all but buried in my throat. His smell, a torrid mix of youth, acrid adolescence, and nervousness, filled my lungs. I expected to hear the restless rains of Antai's winter sweeping walls and windows, and did not.

Mazed for a few moments, I lay perfectly still, my breathing following its accustomed sleep-cycle. If you must, you can train yourself not to change your in-draft or exhale when you wake, a skill much in demand among assassins—or those who would hunt them.

Dreaming. I must be.

D'ri stirred slightly. My arms tensed, and my

stomach. I did not *feel* as if I dreamed. There was a familiar morning pressure in my bladder and another, even more familiar dry rasp of wyrmbreath in my mouth. Sleep-weight crusted my eyes, and Diyan, his knee striking mine, freed himself from my arms with the neutral plaintive muttering of a child who still wishes rest.

No. I thrashed, my elbow sinking into Darik's midriff. He woke with a lunge, and Diyan with a yelp.

"By the Moon—" Darik was already free of the covers and on his feet, a knifeblade glittering as he whirled, searching for the source of the disturbance. I gained my own balance, crouching atop the bed, blankets and linens sliding free, tangling around my ankles.

Diyan clutched at a rolled fur he had been using as a pillow, a thin flexible *stilette* for spearing between ribs gleaming in his own fist. He *had* grown, wrists and ankles far too big for him but showing the promise of the man he would be. His hands were well to catching up, and their knuckles were raw with cold.

"Mother's *tits*," I hissed, "what are *you* doing here?"

The boy rubbed at his own eyes, yawning so wide his back teeth smiled at me. "Ahi-ya, Kaahai, you *scared* me." The cadence of the Freetowns rubbed under his tradetongue, but two Antai loan-words showed where he'd rested, if only briefly. He slipped the *stilette* into the loose sleeve of his dun, coarse-weave sherte, and I stared at his familiar face, broadening at the cheekbones and filling in elsewhere except his pointed chin. His wide dark eyes were the same as always, their folds sharp and handsome.

How was it possible for a child to change so quickly?

I grabbed his shoulders. No longer so thin—at

least he had eaten well, and the cold had not melted flesh from him. Instead, he had *gained* weight. "How. Did you. Get. *Here?*"

"Rode a pig, *cha*." As if it were the most natural thing in the world. "Big long one say tha' fine creatures. Gavvy lutebanger hates 'em, say bad as a ship. Storm was mun, but we—"

"Atyarik?" All strength threatened to leave my legs. "Gavrin? Janaire? *Here?*"

"A'course. Was gonna come mysel', *cha*, and they caught up two days outa Antai. Good thing, too." His smile, wide and trusting, beamed up at me. My hands were claws upon his young shoulders, but he did not seem to mind.

"Kaia." Darik, somewhat slowly, put away his own knife. "Am I dreaming, or are we both?"

"I seem to remember leaving you all safe in Antai," I muttered darkly. "And they…they bring you *here*. By the Moon, I swear I shall—"

"Breakfast!" Diyan bounced on the bed, perhaps to break my hold upon him or to distract me from swearing some manner of vengeance. He, at least, had a healthy regard for my temper. "Big red one say we eat well here, *cha?* Mun fakka last night."

"He still speaks another tongue entirely." Darik addressed the empty air over our foster-son's tousled head. "Now I suspect I am not dreaming. Come, little one, let me look at you. Have you kept your training fresh?"

"Oh, *cha!*" The boy wriggled out of my grasp and off the bed, bare feet landing on cold flooring with a jarring thump. "Long one say I am quick as a farrat. Fat as one, too." He stretched, showing the new length in his arms, expecting our admiration.

I was not disposed to give him aught but a scolding. "D'ri." My tone rivaled the Howl for sharpness. "He says Atyarik, and Janaire—"

"Yes." My *s'tarei* nodded. "I did not think they would lag so far behind, though. Come, Diyan. It is too cold to wander with naked paws."

I settled on my haunches, my feet sinking into the bed's indifferent stuffing. My ankles ached, and the cold had not broken. It had, if anything, intensified.

I had left them safely in Antai. What madness had possessed them to come *here*?

FROM DIYAN'S chatter I learned they had left Antai a few weeks behind us, but where we had led the weather, it had slowed *them*. He was too excited to give many details beyond *bandits* and several references to Atyarik's fascination with *torkascruagh*. There were stories of Janaire calling fire from the air, and several ill-defined "heroics" on Gavrin's part.

Truly, the world had turned upside-down.

The great eating-hall was full of murmurs that morning, and there they were. Janaire, her soft Gavridar face sharper now and vivid with the cold, rose from the bench a moment before Atyarik, severe in his *s'tarei* blank and a great furred black cloak, followed suit. The half-Pesh lutebanger Gavrin, hunched over a massive platter of spiced, ground gutmeat, blinked owlishly when Diyan appeared leading us, a proud shepherd returning two strays to the herd. A new lute-case, not the battered old one, rested upon the bench beside Gavrin, and he was accorded respectful space by the *tain* filling the rest of the table. I could not tell whether the guards were to keep watch on these new arrivals, or had been drawn by Janaire's sleek, beautiful exoticism.

Redfist, for once, was not at Emrath's side but seated across from the G'mai. He rose too, bumping the table, and his grin was the widest I'd seen it since Antai. "K'ai!" he called. "Look what the winds blew in, aye!"

My jaw set so tight it threatened to crack itself; I let D'ri and Diyan precede me. An excited babble rose and swirled, Atyarik clapping D'ri on the shoulder, Diyan ducking under Janaire's arm to accept a half-hug with the ease of long familiarity. It was Gavrin who watched me solemnly, his uneasy half-Pesh complexion paling. Jorath Blacknose sat on the other side of Gavrin's lute-case, and his gaze, following our minstrel's, was disconcertingly direct.

They looked...well. Atyarik was a little leaner and more somber, and Janaire's G'mai dresses were covered by layers of wool and fur, and Gavrin's sleeves, of course, were a little too short. Later, I learned it was he who had taken the lead, for the Skaialan hold bards in high honor if they have any skill at all, considering them sacred to Kroth's youngest brother whose strange flat unbellied lute makes the wind rise or fall. Even their bandits will often let a lutebanger go in peace with enough supplies to reach the next settlement.

Kaia? D'ri's inner voice, reaching me over a great distance. A great white wasteland opened inside me, to match the one without. He glanced back at me, but the others had claimed his attention, and he was too well-bred not to greet a fellow *s'tarei* and *adai*.

A hush fell, or perhaps I simply stopped hearing the slurping, banging, jesting, shouting that is the Skaialan at their meals. The fire took none of the stone-chill away, merely blunted its edge a fraction. I watched Diyan's mouth move, Darik listening close as Atyarik and Janaire spoke rapidly, no doubt telling of their journey and its many wonders. My arms crossed over my chest, my fingers digging through layers to almost bruise my biceps, I held Gavrin's gaze for a few heartbeats. He chewed, thoughtfully, and when the silence descended around me, it was a relief.

I turned and left the eating-hall. A half-candle-mark later, crunching through snow that had not been swept from the keep's battlements, I watched as a long dark snake worked its way down the northern road, spreading to encompass the arm Kalburn had lain across that trade-route. Banners, pulled taut in a stinging wind that whipped snow from the ground and rasped it against every surface, were black blots with strange snarling crimson blood-spots caught upon their folds.

My merry troupe of outcasts had stupidly followed us into the jaws of a Highland winter. And Dunkast, the Ferulaine with his witchery, his unholy gem, and his intent to kill Rainak Redfist had arrived as well.

TAKING KALBURN TOO

WHEN THE LADY of Kalburn receives an envoy, she does so in her great hall under the massive, wax- and tallow-dripping chandelier. If it is one of her vassals with business, a few of the *tain* most closely connected to the affair by kinship or interest will be in attendance; if it is a matter to be judged, only those *unconnected* are brought into the hall, to protect their lady from outbursts of temper and the claimants from rending each other in her presence. This time, Emrath Needleslay was receiving her husband, and rows of *tain* faced outward before her dais. She sat upon her stone bench, straight-backed, the same blue stone ear-drops glittering alongside her neck and a heavy torc of their pale gold clasped about the high collar of her fine indigo dress, its great mantle worked with bright sunny embroidery inside its lapels and floor-brushing sleeves. Her golden hair, the top half braided into a crown and the lower into a complex rope that reached her hips, glinted.

To her right, his ruddy arms crossed over his barrel chest, Redfist glowered. He had made no attempt at fineness of costume today, and it was just as well.

Torches flared along the walls, an extravagance in the middle of the day. Either that, or Emrath wanted all the light she could cast upon her husband. A cunning system of highly polished trash-metal discs tilted at precise angles in honeycomb passages brings light into many interior rooms of Kalburn's keep, but the overcast today prevented much of their effectiveness.

I kept to the shadows along the left-hand wall. D'ri and the other G'mai, tightly grouped, were behind the first row of *tain* on the right side of the steps. I made no attempt to join them, despite D'ri's sudden, painful attention blooming in the deep spaces of the *taran'adai*.

If there was to be violence, he would defend the others. I had other plans.

We waited perhaps a quarter-candlemark, while Dunkast, who had been greeted at the keep's great door by Emrath, cooled his heels in the hall outside like any other supplicant. Emrath did not speak, nor did Redfist, and the *tain* rustled and shifted with whispers.

Finally, the Needleslay stirred, and nodded. Her *tain* took a collective breath, and I studied their faces from my vantage point. All pasty, most bearded—Jorath Blacknose was an exception, and there were one or two others—and, to a man, stiff-necked. The whites of their eyes showed a little too wide; their hands were too tight upon sword or axe-hilt. The flail-users, useless in even this broad space, carried two single-axes apiece, and looked sour at the change.

I knew the slight metallic aroma that clung to their *keltas* and sour sweat, to their clenched jaws and white knuckles.

Fear.

The two *tain* at the double door reached for large vertical handles, and pulled, muscles flickering in their bare calves. A silhouette in the widening doorway was neither monstrous nor twisted, and that was the first surprise.

The second was that he was not tall, nor overly broad. Among the giants of the North he was merely average, and I might have expected him to move with the bantiness of a fowl who knows his size and must compensate with the willingness to attack first. Instead, he stepped quietly, flanked only by two of his own *tain*, both a half-head larger than him and dark-haired in red-and-yellow *keltas*.

Dunkast the Ferulaine was neither dark nor blond, but somewhere between. His gaze was bright blue, though, much brighter than Redfist's, and there was something in the shape of his jaw reminiscent of my giant ginger-furred friend. He carried no weapon, and neither did his two *tain*, but neither of his guards seemed nervous at all.

He paused a bare five paces inside the door, passing his gaze over the hall, unhurried. I drew further back into an angle where the torchlight did not reach, and my hand ached for a hilt, any hilt.

The thing, the witched gem he had found in some Northern cave or tomb, sat upon his chest, plainly visible since he wore no cloak or over-mantle despite the cold.

Its back had been carved flat to rest against its wearer, and its curved front cut with facets I could not count at a glance, each one apparently a different size. Its chain, of heavy black metal, became paler near the stone's glittering setting, for either the jewelsmith had known some art for fusing metal to carven stone links, or the black clot held in the setting was spreading mineral fingers through its prison.

Either prospect sent a cool trickle of dread down my spine.

His scrape-shaven cheeks were ruddy, but not, as the rest of the Skaialans', from the cold. Instead, it seemed a surfeit of blood surged under his pale Northern skin, and his lips were rubescent too, like a Rijiin courtesan's carmine mouth. I looked closer— the roots of his hair were lighter than the tips, and *that* was exceedingly odd. The sun had not bleached those strands, nor had an honest wind.

I studied the gem, too. It did not *look* witched, but then, I was no judge of such things.

At least, I had not been before Darik had brought himself to upend my life. Still, I felt nothing but my own silence, the quiet of an assassin lying in wait. Redfist, on the dais, inhaled sharply, silently.

Dunkast finished his survey of the hall. His reddened lips twitched, sardonic amusement plucking at their raw edges. I restrained the urge to draw back further; my hip already brushed the stone wall. *An adder under a rock knows only patience*, the Thieves' Guild says.

I wondered briefly how many nights Sorche Smahua's-kin spent lying in shadow-wait, dreaming of striking me down. When you know what your quarry looks like, it is easy to fill your skull with imagining their death, in various permutations. Sometimes it may even be a comfort, or a means of discerning where one's plans may go awry. Like every habit of dreaming while awake, it has its drawbacks.

You may imagine your enemy's death, and it leads naturally to imagining your own.

"Needleslay." Dunkast Ferulaine's voice was neither high nor low. Simply…average, like the rest of him. It was passing strange, and I stilled even further. The gem…it did not reflect a gleam, from mirrorlight *or* flame. "Ye be keeping ill company in my absence, wife."

No, any light simply fell into the black eye upon the Ferulaine's chest. Fell…or was eaten, trapped below those facets.

Consumed.

Redfist looked ready to stride from the dais and challenge him immediately, but it was Emrath who spoke, clear and measured, her back straight and her skirts arranged as beautifully as a G'mai girl's. "All of Kalburn saw him strike the Anvil, Ferulaine."

Dunkast Ferulaine's gaze fell upon Janaire and the two *s'tarei* with her upon the dais steps. "Perhaps his elvish witched it."

Would *everyone* in this frozen, uncivilized waste-land use that gods-be-damned word? I kept myself so still I barely breathed, air filtering into and out of my lungs with the silence of a calm sea slow-lapping a choke-sand shore.

"Ye think Kroth Himself so weak as to allow witching?" Emrath's laugh held no amusement, but a great deal of contempt. *Her* jewels glittered, and so did her eyes, a hard gleam. There was steel in the Lady of Kalburn, and it needed only a strike against her edge to show the spark. "Or is that what *ye* planned to do, if I could be forced to walk to the Stones at your side?"

"And the man ye walked instead is hiding behind yer *tain* and yer skirts." Dunkast's faint smile stretched, as a night-hunting eyebird will open its beak. "I see him standing there. Hello, Rainak."

"Dunkast." Redfist shook his head. "Ye've changed. Again."

My hand crept for my *dotani* hilt. The light-drinking gem…something about the setting teased at memory and intuition both. My eyes half-closed, vision sharpening. When you see something you know but do not expect, miles away from any place it should be, it is easy to convince yourself your own senses are lying. The Shainakh call it *mind-that-balks*, and the last word can also be applied to a horse that will not do as it's told.

Kaahai.

"Not so much." Dunkast's hand lifted. His fingertips were reddened too, and the cool trickle of dread down my back turned to a river of shiverflesh.

Three sinuous carven lines, knotted and re-knotted, over and over again, nestled around the gem's blind, hungry eye. Of course it was familiar. The only question was, how had it traveled this far North? Oh, it was *possible*, I supposed. More than possible. Suddenly, the floury paleness of the giants here held an altogether more sinister cast.

What if, instead of not deigning to go north to conquer the savage barbarians, the Pensari had instead…moved *south*? Or perhaps a remnant of them *had* gone north, fleeing the curse and wrack of all their kin, leaving their treasures in a cold cave to be pawed over by barbarians?

"Not so much," Dunkast repeated, his blushing fingertips stroking the gem's setting. For a moment, the undulating triple-line knots seemed to move, following his caress. "I was always thus. Ye did not see it. And neither did *he*."

Redfist surged forward, his *kelta* swinging angrily. The *tain* parted for him, and I tensed. But he stopped a few paces beyond their last row, and faced Dunkast over empty flagstones scattered with rush and sweetstraw, moisture collecting in the corners from our collective breath and the earth's own heat rising from *skauna* and deep earthfire shafts below.

Our great, ruddy barbarian held his once-brother's blue gaze, and his own was hot with fury. "How did ye kill him, Dunkast? Poison? Or did ye sneak into his tent and strangle him before yer bastards attacked in the dark? Our *father*."

"He was no father to me." Dunkast smiled outright, the surfaces of his lips cracking as if he was desert-dry. The ice can steal moisture from you as well as vital heat, but the canyons in his mouthflesh did not bleed, for all they were vivid crimson. "He was a red-eyed buggering fool, and deserved his fate."

Redfist pitched forward, and for a moment I thought the battle-rage would take him and we would have an end to the whole affair in short order. I shifted my own weight, my hand closing about my *dotani* hilt and the decision bending my left knee —first, I would take the Ferulaine *tain* on the right, a *piri*-splitter strike to drive him back and if it opened his throat, so much the better. The one to the left I would have to lunge for, and much would depend on whether or not he had a weapon hidden in his *kelta*.

Striking down the unarmed, and a guest of this household besides, did not particularly bother me at the moment. Not with that hideous *thing* upon Dunkast's chest, its alien gaze sharpening as if it sensed bloodshed approaching and liked the thought. The Ferulaine's head tilted slightly and his pupils swelled, swallowing the blue of his irises as his chin made a strange, fluid motion, his neck moving subtly as if full of fluid, instead of a column of stacked bone and strap-muscles. "Ah." Those pupils swiveled to point in my general direction, and his head made another strange little movement. "There is your witchling bitch. A man who keeps more than one woman loses all of them, Rainak."

"My companion is a *wal'kir*, come from Kroth himself to watch me take your head." Redfist's throat filled with a wet, grinding noise, and he spat. The gobbet, flung a fair distance, splattered on the rushes just before Dunkast's boots.

The Skaialan hold such a thing to be a grave insult indeed.

"I challenge ye, Dunkast Ferulaine." Redfist did not take another step, but his tone drove the other man heel-back, rocking upon the latter portion of his boots, for it was cold as the White Howl itself. "Ye shall answer for accusing me of kinslaying, for yer crimes, and for that *thing* you wear, unholy in Krom's sight. Tomorrow, at noon, on the Great Ground of Kalburn. Now get ye gone, and trouble my lady Needleslay no more."

"Your *lady* Needleslay is my wife—" The bland amusement had left Dunkast, and his pupils shrank again. Whatever he had expected, it was not this. A rippling murmur went through the assembled Kalburn *tain*, and the gem's setting had ceased its twitching. Some other current filled the room, fey and crackling, and I did not need to look at the dais-steps to know it was Janaire, her dark, beautiful eyes wide and Atyarik's hand to her shoulder, who provided that clarifying force.

"You are merely *talanach*," Redfist said. "And after I take yer head I shall be taking Kalburn, too." He used a particularly pungent Skaialan verb for coupling, one used to describe rutting beasts, and a shiver of distaste went through me. Emrath Needleslay colored, but I had no time to worry for her or her pride, for one of the Ferulaine *tain* slid his hand below the third of his *kelta* flung over his middle and shoulder, and my *dotani* half-leapt from its sheath. The small sliding noise broke the tension, and Dunkast merely glanced in my direction, perhaps not even seeing me clearly, before turning and shoving between his two guards, passing from the Great Hall of Kalburn like a poisonous, invisible gas draining away.

For the first time Redfist had seen the man in five years, it went tolerably well, I thought.

I was wrong, for more than one reason.

STRIKE THE WEAK

THE NEEDLESLAY SWEPT from the Great Hall after giving a few crisp orders in Skaialan, and Redfist hurried in her wake. I followed, my stride lengthening and my head a-whirl. I might have caught Redfist and dragged him aside, had Darik's hand not closed about my elbow hard enough to pull me to a halt. "Kaia! Are you well?" Behind him, Janaire was pale under her copper coloring, her *s'tarei*'s long Tyaanismir face almost as bloodless as he held her upright, his arms about her waist. No sign of Gavrin or Diyan in the hall, thank the Moon.

"Well enough." I pulled against his hold, dismissing the two G'mai—Atyarik was more than capable of caring for his *adai*, and now that I had seen Dunkast and his gem, there was much to be done. "I must speak to—"

Darik did not let go. A flush spread along his high, blade-sharp cheekbones. "That *thing* he wears struck Janaire. It is *dangerous*."

Did he think me unaware of the peril? "It's Pensari, *of course* it's dangerous." Irritated, I plucked at his fingers. "Turn loose of me, D'ri, I must speak with Redfist."

"*She* needs you more than he does, *adai*." His face set, as if an unpleasant smell drifted by. His G'mai was sharp, and its inflection perilously close to chastisement. "Must I beg you?"

Wait. "It *struck* her?" I repeated his phrase, hoping I had misunderstood. "Is that what you said?"

"Yes, *adai'mi*." The faint unsteadiness was his, trembling inside his bone-channels and spilling into me. "I thought it might have touched you too."

"No, of course not." I almost added, *I have enough wit to avoid being witched*, but it was ill-tempered of me, and untrue besides. "Perhaps he thought her…" *Perhaps he thought her* me? *At least at first?*

"She requires an *adai's* care, Kaia." Again, as if I were an idiot.

I could not blame him. Such a request was, of course, more important than speaking to a mere barbarian, and no doubt he wondered at my tardiness. I shook free of Darik's grasp, finally, and pierced the crowd of milling *tain* with long swinging strides. "*Yada'Adais.*" It was little trouble to find the most honorific inflection. "What ails you?"

Chalky, trembling, she peered at me as she would a stranger, and Atyarik's arms tightened about her. "That *thing*," he said, curtly, "is dangerous."

So we have established. "I am well aware." They had been here for less than a day, and already I was well past irritated and upon the road to anger.

Atyarik's long lean face set against itself. "And you did not think to warn another *adai*?"

That would be a heavy charge indeed. "I did not know what it *was*, until I saw it. I am exactly as surprised as you, Tyaanismir."

He cut my explanation short, his inflection killing-sharp. "Then do you know how to treat her?"

"I…" I examined her more closely. Her breathing was high and shallow, her lips drained of color. "What *happened*?"

"The thing sought to use *ba'narak'n'adai*." His mouth twisted with distaste. With good reason; the stealing of another's will was one of the most abhorrent acts possible with Power.

"Mother Moon." I peeled up one of her eyelids, conscious of my practice-chapped and cold-roughened skin against the soft fineness of hers. The lowland G'mai are not bred of mountain-bone, and of all the Blessed, their beauty is the least harsh. Her pupils flickered, swelling and shrinking, and a fine, misty dampness lay upon her copper skin. "Oh. Ah."

"*Help* her!" Atyarik was sweating too; the word was sharp, cut short in the imperative, but the lift in the middle made it a plea.

There was no time for gentleness, and in any case, I have none of that quality. So, I did the only thing I could think of.

I slapped her.

Not too softly, either, for a half-measure is worse than a double when it comes to thumping a fellow sellsword back into her skin and away from battleshock, but with nowhere near my full strength. Her head snapped aside, the crack of the blow slicing through the shuffle-murmurs of the *tain*, and if Atyarik had not been so busy holding his *adai* to her feet, he might have struck me in return. As it was, he jerked as if I had hit him as well, and sense flooded Janaire's dark gaze. She sagged in his grasp, her hands lifting—fluttering doves, helplessly flickering to drive away a pursuer.

"Come back," I rasped, in deliberately harsh G'-mai. "*Back* into yourself, *lya-ini*."

It was the first time I had called her *age-mate*, and perhaps that was what stopped Atyarik from dropping her and drawing his *dotanii*. That, and Darik's hand biting my shoulder, fingers digging in cruelly as he spun me about, my balance on the third dais step grown precarious.

"What have you *done?*" my *s'tarei* hissed, and I realized, perhaps a moment too late, that striking an *adai* is a great crime. Of course it would shock them both.

But it was only and fully what was necessary. Janaire reeled, shuddered, and clasped her palm to her reddening cheek, wonderingly, staring. "Kaia?" she whispered, a bare breath passing her lips as they shaped the word.

"Aye, *lya-ini*. Come back to your skin and bone, I have not time to nurse you." I nodded and changed to tradetongue, harsh after the song of G'mai. "*That* is what I have done, princeling. And if you do not take your hand from me I shall strike *you*, not nearly as softly."

His grasp fell away, I nodded to Janaire, spun, and took to my heels.

∼

I MANAGED to track Redfist and Emrath by following the shouting.

"Ye're a great fool, Rainak, and ye ever have been. Ye think you shall be *taking Kalburn*, too? Is that so?" She was capable of great sonorousness, the Lady of Kalburn, and used every inch of it.

Redfist was not precisely quiet himself, but at least he was seeking to explain and not to overpower. "Emrath, twas said to unsettle—"

"Was it now?" Emrath apparently thought little of his tactics. "All of ye, the same! Men, men, *men*, thinking a woman no better than a *kelta* to wipe with! No, not even a *kelta*, for ye prize yer colors boldly, do ye all!"

For once, I was in complete agreement with the grey-eyed queenling of Kalburn. I closed the heavy wooden door, fitted into an alcove some distance from the Great Hall's entrance, and leaned against it. This chamber was no doubt for a guest or supplicant to wait within, perhaps for hours at a time; dark wooden benches ringed it, and the reflected light was weak and wavering. Tapestries, all colorful and some very fine, curtained dusty stone; there was no fireplace, and only a cold, empty brazier in the middle of the room broke the monotony of the naked flags, no sweetstraw or rushes scattered to cushion bare stone. The *tain* were not in the admittedly small and cramped hallway outside the door, but I thought it only a matter of time before servant and guard alike clotted wherever they could hear raised voices.

Emrath rounded on Redfist, her fists clenched, high color staining her usually-pale cheeks. Grey eyes snapping, drawn up to her full regal height, glowing with rage, she was…well, not as beautiful as my darling Clau Kesa at the Swallows Moon, but very fetching indeed even with uncooked dough for skin. "Ye could have challenged him without smirching me, Rainak, and ye chose not to. Just as ye chose to leave me to his clutches."

"Ye did not complain!" Redfist parried, his tone rising to match hers and his red-tinged hands knotted into fists.

"I wished ye to *live*!" Emrath fair screamed it, and I crossed my arms, my palm stinging. Perhaps striking Janaire had not been the *best* solution, but it had been effective. I had little skill in the use of Power, and if the gem or the things it made in the shape of men were so dangerous to an *adai* using an *adai's* gifts, well, other methods were called for.

It was only now it occurred to me that perhaps both all three G'mai would not see my logic. But Mother's *tits*, the witless, blundering castoffs had followed me to this place, and now I was tasked with not only watching Redfist's back—a proposition I was beginning to think somewhat large for even *my* talents—but corralling and protecting *them* as well. Which leaving them in Antai had been to *avoid*.

I do not deny a certain satisfaction in slapping the Gavridar, either. Perhaps, if I were to be absolutely, strictly, and fully honest, I only regretted I could not repeat the act upon *all* of them, stem to stern, and perhaps force some sense in through the blows. If they were to attach themselves to me, was it too much to ask that they would stay where I placed them, where I could be reasonably certain they were safe?

And how many times had I repeated to myself, *at least the others are in Antai, and not suffering this?*

"I wished ye to live," Emrath repeated, losing some of her volume but none of her force. "I sold myself to yon bastard to keep my people safe, and to keep your trail clear. And what do ye do, *Connaight Crae*? Throw mud upon me, at every turn."

"I could have brought ye, Emrath!" Redfist had well and truly lost any desire to restrain his voice. His bellow was almost a battlefield-shout. "We could have made a fine life in the underlands, away from this!"

"How far do ye think I could travel to escape the Stones?" She regarded him as a laundress might a stubborn stain upon fine material, her chin up and her hands knotted to match his. They were indeed a fine pair. "I am *Kalburn*, Rainak! Kroth himself cannae undo that chain, and taken from the Stones I wither." Her shoulders sagged, crushed by an invisible weight, a feeling I knew all too well. "Great bloody bairns, the lot of ye. If I could escape to the underlands, aye, I would, but not in *thy* company."

Breathless silence. Emrath clapped her hand over her mouth, the double marriage-ring glittering.

Redfist stepped forward, his arm lifting, and I realized he meant to strike her. From his stance, it would not be a love-tap, or even a shock-breaker.

"Are you twain finished with your courting?" Deliberately loud, deliberately crude, my Skaialan jarred them both. "There are more weighty matters before us, idiots."

It might have been amusing to see them realize another was watching their display, if not for Redfist's half-turn towards me, his great ham-fists clenched and his face suffused with ugly ruddiness. "K'ai! Ye little sneaking—"

"Be very careful how you end that sentence, friend Redfist." I crossed my arms, my *dotani* a comforting weight upon my back and each knife upon me easy in its sheath. "I know what your once-brother Dunkast carries, Rainak Redfist, and we must speak. Else I would leave you to your business here, and tend to my own."

Emrath, perhaps unsurprisingly, did not think much of my interruption either. "I have had enough of ye." Her grey eyes all but spat sparks, and she hissed like a cat seeking a mate upon a Hain balcony in the dead of summer, when every touch against sweating skin is an irritation and fur double the burden. "Were ye not my guest, *susnach* whore, I would have ye scourged and driven from Kalburn."

"No doubt." I showed my teeth, and it was not a smile. "*If* you had any among your *tain* who could match me, Skaialan queenling, for I would not go quietly as long as my friends were in danger."

That halted her.

"K'ai." Redfist sighed, his rage draining as wine from an empty skin. "Can ye not be graceful, for *once?*"

"Ask yourself that before me, barbarian." It boggled the mind, that he was seeking to chide *me* for ill behavior. "In *my* country a man does not strike his lover." They had no word for *adai*, and did not seem to feel the lack. "In any case, your Dunkast has found a bit of Pensari witchery, and Janaire kept it from turning the entire room into snarling dogs fighting over your entrails. You should thank her, and prettily too for it drove her into shock that might have stoppered her breath entire."

"Pensari?" He repeated the word, incomprehension coloring its syllables.

"Do your people have no word for them? That is strange indeed." I shook my head. History was not our quandary now; the bards could fight over exactly where the light-eating jewel came from at leisure after its danger was met and surpassed, and Dunkast Ferulaine neutralized in one manner or another. "Come. Let us go where there is at least a fire, and speak of it. You have challenged him, you should know what you are fighting."

They regarded me as if I had suddenly grown another head, or begun speaking in an ancient incomprehensible tongue.

Finally, Redfist unclenched his fists, and his battle-readiness faded. "Very well. Step outside, K'ai. I would speak to the Needleslay some little more."

"Do that." I paused. "But keep your hands off the lady Needleslay, Redfist. It is beneath you to strike the weak."

I had thought Emrath would be grateful. The look she shot me was anything but.

CHILDREN OR SLAVES

IF IT WAS a council of war, it was an exceeding uncomfortable one. Janaire, the mark on her face
swiftly fading, kept glancing nervously at me. Atyarik, fuming, stood behind her chair—it was not the
first time he thought me a sad excuse for an *adai*, and
I knew it would not be the last. Darik stood behind
my own seat, but otherwise did not acknowledge me.
Gavrin, his dark hair rumpled into a harpy's nest, sat
next to Jorak Blacknose, since bards are the reposito-
ries of history and lore in whatever land they find
themselves. Redfist did not look at Emrath, who was
bloodless and almost silent at the head of the great
table.

A few more of her *tain* attended as well, two
blond giants and a dark one. The dark one—Emrath's
High Steward, Korbrin Brightbock—was grey-griz-
zled and lean for a Skaialan, and an iron archer's ring
sat upon his right thumb. He rubbed at its carving,
meditatively, and his gaze was just as quick and
sharply intelligent as Blacknose's.

The blonds blurred into each other; many Skaialan look the same to me. But one was the high-cap-
tain of the *tain*, and the other a *blesagathk*—a priest

sworn to one of their gods, one who married and rode to war like the followers of the Hain butterfly goddess who, every six of their thousand-summer cycles, changes from female to male, or back again. She is the patron of acrobats and those who fight in the pits, and the Hain hold the Moon to be her lamp, lifted as she traverses the halls of night searching for her breasts when she is female or her shaft while he is male.

"He rode to battle against the blue tribes," Blacknose said heavily. "And came back with the gem. Some say he found it in a tomb, or that the chieftain he fought had it in an iron casket."

"A tomb is more likely." I spread my hands upon the tabletop and studied them. "Perhaps some Pensari who escaped the ruin came this far North. Though the Anhedrin hold that their last Khana retreated south. I do not know."

"Tell us of these Pensari." Korbrin, the steward, addressed the words over my head, as if he expected D'ri to speak.

I cast through mental storehouses, arranging what I had been told. "The Anhedrin called them *the travelers*. They were said to come from elsewhere. They were pale, but ruddy at lip and fingertip, and they worshipped death." A blood-bubble under my left firstfinger's nail was a reminder of daily sword-drill. Janaire's hands were much softer, and unmarked, laying decorous in her lap as she studied me, quick intelligence in her dark gaze. "They had their witchery, brought out of the Sundering when their home was shattered. Though they may have *come* from the North, who knows? Your kind are certainly pale enough."

"It matters little where he got the thing *from*," one of the blonds—the head-captain, Sorek Piercefoot—

remarked. "He used to only wear it in battle. But he brought it into the Great Hall, before the Needleslay."

"*Ba'narak'n'adai.*" Janaire shuddered, her G'mai soft with loathing. "He wanted them to become as dogs. Wild dogs, and to kill our big red barbarian."

Korbrin's expression darkened. "What does she say?"

I had to pause, to find the right words in Skaialan and the slurry of trade-tongue, to be as precise as possible. "She is a teacher among the G'mai, and knows much of the shapes Power may take. She says your Dunkast was seeking to use the stone to rob the assembled of their will and turn them upon Redfist. To tear him apart like dogs after entrails."

A tiny movement of revulsion went through the Steward, echoed by every other Skaialan. Gavrin opened his mouth, shut it, and shot me a furtive glance.

"Well?" I prompted.

"Nothing." But all gazes were focused on him, now. His Skaialan was halting, so he used tradetongue instead. "I heard a lay, in Antai, of the Khana Alhai's fall. Tis sung he sent treasures north, to keep them from the hands of the slum-citizens who threatened his throne."

"Ah." I nodded. It made sense, though why would a king send his treasure where he did not intend to follow? "Perhaps. In any case, the thing is carved with a Pensari word, over and over."

The steward regarded me narrowly. "And which word would that be?"

"Death." I used the Skaialan, so there could be no misunderstanding, but my left hand still jumped to an *avert* sign. When speaking of the Pensari, it is always best to be cautious. "And you said he was dark before, Redfist. The thing is...*bleaching* him."

"And he stinks of the sorcerous urine used, no doubt." Redfist addressed himself to Korbrin. "Still think me a kinslayer and a liar, Steward?"

The dark Skaialan's jaw hardened. "I think ye a selfish brat, Rainak Redfist. *That* has not changed."

"Ye may duel over such words later," Emrath broke in. "Tell us, Lady Gemerh." The Skaialan approximation of *G'mai* she addressed to Janaire, and quite respectfully, too. "What may be done to break this witched gem?"

"Break it?" Korbrin did not let Janaire speak.

Emrath regarded him steadily. "Aye. Without it, he is simply another clan leader, one who has not made many friends. And his Black Brothers, too—breaking the gem means he may not make *more*." An impatient movement of her shoulders—she was used to the men around her being slow to the point, and for a moment I felt for her. "Or it may rob the ones he has of their cursed life. So, tell us, Lady Gemerh. How may we fight or destroy that thing?"

All eyes rested upon the Gavridar now. Janaire colored slightly, glancing at me. Her tradetongue might not be equal to the task.

"Speak in whatever tongue you wish." I hoped I wore an encouraging expression, and nodded. "Anything you may tell them would be a great help, *Yada'Adais*. I will translate, should you have difficulty."

"I do not know much," she began in G'mai, her inflection soft and troubled. "It is a blasphemous thing, to steal the will from another; it is a blasphemous thing to create such an artifact. It sought to control the whole room, but your silence—Kaia, it is like a *s'tarei*'s—choked it. So I was able to turn the force back on itself. Otherwise...I would not have been troubled overmuch by it, because of *s'tarei'mi*." Behind her chair, Atyarik straightened perceptibly. Her hand crept upward; his found her shoulder, and they drew both visibly drew comfort from the touch. "But the others? Yes, they would have fallen victim, and even your silence or your sword might not have held them. So. The means of making such an artifact—"

"What does she say?" The blond *blesagathk* drummed his meaty fingers upon the tabletop as the fire—a mighty mound of blackrock, putting out what heat it could—made a whispering sound. The priest's nose was the same shape as the other blond's, and I thought them perhaps related.

"When she is finished, I will *tell* you," I snapped, then shifted to G'mai again. "Forgive the barbarian's rudeness, *Yada'Adais*. You were saying?"

Janaire's eyes glistened. Was she about to weep? "Oh, now you are so *polite*." Her hand tensed upon Atyarik's, and the Tyaanismir glared at me. "To make such a thing, much Power must be wedded to a physical thing. A sticking-post." The word was for a spike driven deep to hobble a restive horse, but her inflection stripped it of any double meaning. "Break the physical thing, and the Power will drain away from its shards over time. Yet it may resist fracture, since Power strengthens, and if it is broken, it may take a long while to lose its potency."

I translated as well as I could, Skaialan and tradetongue, sometimes repeating myself in both to make certain of precision. Emrath steepled her fingers before her face, and her grey eyes half-lidded as she settled in her chair. This aspect of her—calm, thoughtful, and distant—was new.

"Oh, what I'd give for Kroth's other hammer," Jorath Blacknose finally said, when I made it clear I was finished. Every Skaialan present smiled; it was part of one of their proverbs.

"So I fight him tomorrow at noon." Redfist dropped his fist on the table, but gently, thoughtfully, punctuation instead of pounding. "The Gemerh keep his blasted gem from aiding him, and when we are done, we take the hideous thing and pound it to pieces with the hammer at the Stones."

"It may not be that simple." I dispelled the urge to swing my feet, since they barely touched the floor, and my thoughtfulness matched Emrath's. The change in this particular battlefield was not a good one. "He did not expect the gem to be countered, and now he is wary *and* warned."

"Aye." Emrath pressed her fingers together harder, knuckle and fingertip whitening together. Her stillness was almost an assassin's. "If he sends his Black Brothers, we may all be dead in our beds come morn. Or if they second him tomorrow—"

"I shall have the Gemerh men second me." Redfist said it as if it were already decided. "They are canny fighters, are they not? And proof to such things?"

"If they agree," I pointed out, mildly. "Janaire may not wish to risk her *s'tarei* in such a fashion, Redfist, and I am not certain I wish to risk mine." *Especially against those...things.* "If need be, *I* shall second you. But are you so certain he will tamely walk to the dancing-ground?" For *I* was not, and the more I considered the situation, the more I thought knifing the man before he could cause more mischief was the less honorable but more *effective* path.

And once I elicited any information about where he was likely to rest this eve, I could begin the work immediately.

"Kaia—" Darik subsided when I tensed, but his quiet promised trouble as soon as we were alone.

Korbrin's laughter, rich and deep, took us all by surprise. "She speaks as a *wal'kir* indeed, this one."

The edge to the words was not polite, nor helpful, and the steward regarded me balefully.

"Picked my pocket in a city full of little men, and I've not been free of her since." Redfist glowered, but not at him. "Lass, in the Highlands, women are not seconds. Dunkast will—"

"I care little what he thinks, or your barbarian countrymen." My temper, firmly reined since I awoke that morning, was sadly frayed. "You were *my* second not so long ago, Rainak Redfist, and I shall thank you to let me return the favor. If you like, it will make us quits and you will be *free of me.*" I could not push the massive chair back quickly enough; my heels would not reach the floor. I felt D'ri's hurried move aside. "Or before you fight Dunkast, I will call you to the dueling circle myself, to teach you not to treat me as one of your trammeled sows."

"Kaia—" Janaire began, faintly.

"And *you*," I interrupted, rounding upon her. It felt better to be on my feet instead of lost in a too-big chair, a doll or child forgotten after a feast. "I left you safe in Antai, with enough gold to get you all through the winter. What possessed you to bring your *s'tarei* and a child, and that blasted lutebanger, into this manner of danger?"

"This blasted lutebanger would have come anyway," Gavrin retorted hotly, clipping the end from my question. "You are not my mother, Kaia Steelflower, and I was manumit before I met you. We are not your children *or* your slaves."

I paused, my hand resting upon the high, peaked chair-back. Silence crawled through the room, underscored only by the snap and pop of burning in the fireplace. Weak light gilded each edge, already dying in the corners.

The nights are hungry in the winter Highlands,

and they eat half the day. "Very well," I began, and the Moon Herself witness me, I was on the verge of saying something irredeemable.

Perhaps it was a blessing I did not have the chance. There was a series of splintering knocks upon the door, and one of Emrath's *tain*—a weedy young man just past his axe-gifting—burst in. Had he not been instantly recognizable, I do not doubt one or more of those present might have sent steel into his guts, one way or another; a general movement of hand to hilt or haft and chairs pushed back almost swallowed his first words.

"Fire!" he gasped. "Ferulaine. The walls. *Fire!*"

DUNKAST FERULAINE DID NOT INTEND to meet Rainak Redfist in single combat. Instead, he had brought not only *his* clan, but the other "bastard" ones from the fringes of Highlands, eking out a living on the wastelands none of the others wanted. They flocked to his banner, expecting a greater place at the councils of the Highlands, full votes instead of half. They believed he would grant it, for those who hewed to him before he was King in truth.

And if they had to break Kalburn's city and keep to rid their chieftain of the one man—not to mention the wife— who looked likely halt Dunkast's plans, they would do their best.

HIS GREAT LUMPEN SELF

WHEN THEY SING of siege and battle, many are the things left out of quatrain and melody. Like the screams of those trapped in burning houses, the cries of those who run from the inferno only to be cut down by the blood-minded or battle-mad, or the sweetish roasting scent of burned people-flesh and the brass note of death upon a great scale settling over a battlefield like folded, feathered wings.

The trade-arms and slums of Kalburn outside the Old City's walls were aflame. When the wind veered, it carried a breath of burning upon its icy back as well as that brass-note, and the faint skirling echoes of death dealt to those who carry no blades as well. Horns sounded at each Old City gate—the *tain* in charge of the walls had reacted swiftly, for the Lady of Kalburn had given orders that the Old City was to be sealed as soon as her erstwhile husband left that morn. Massive gates, creaking and groaning, had shut almost in the face of the first band of screaming Skaialan, their faces smeared with chalky paint, who attempted to take the guard-house at the northern-most one.

Unfortunately, the East Gate, facing the road to

the Standing Stones, was not quick enough. We did not know *exactly* what had happened there, since the *tain* responsible for its guarding did not survive.

Often afterwards I thought upon it, and decided Dunkast had given his orders early too. A fighting withdrawal through an old Skaialan city with narrow, winding cobbled ways was underway. When it approached the Keep itself, then I could do some good. The Old City roiled like a poked anthill inside its stone skirting.

I stood next to Redfist on the battlements of Kalburn Keep, both of us wrapped against the wind. His blue gaze fixed north and his beard catching small flakes of blowing snow, he was a welcome windbreak, but his wrinkled brow spelled worry in characters as plain-spiked as Skaialan scratch-writing. "She suspected this," he said, finally. "Canny girl."

So far, Emrath Needleslay was a length ahead of any pursuer. It remained to see whether she could win the race, or if she were a hare doomed to the stew-pot. "Tis no great trick to plan for the worst." I sank my chin into the fur collar of a quilted, lined jacket. My ear-tips were miserably cold again. "Did you think he would face you honorably, then?"

"The challenge was issued in front of the *tain*." Redfist shook his red-furred head. It seemed he could not, even after this, compass his once-brother's treachery. "Is he mad? The clans will—"

I thought he simply wished someone else to say the obvious, so he could hear the terrain as well as see its hollows and peaks. Often a general needs an *adjii* to do so, and this was, after all, *his* land. So I obliged, as I had more than once for Ammerdahl Rikyat or a ship-captain who had earned my aid. "If he kills *you*, do you think any from the others will take your place? He cannot kill Emrath directly, but at this point, pouring her a poisoned cup might suit his purposes even better." It was relatively easy to place myself in Dunkast's position and simply think, *what would I do, were I aiming only to win?*

Relatively, and *disturbingly,* easy.

Redfist said nothing. He simply glared at the battle, leaned forward, a racing-dog denied the chance to run.

I decided to turn to more productive matters. There was nothing to be done for anyone outside the Old City. "How long will it take other clans to travel here?" Even if they did so, how many of them would come to Emrath's aid? Or Redfist's? I did not know enough of this strange country's politics yet, and exhaled hard against mounting frustration.

"In winter? Hard to say. Travel is slow, and the treecrack is nigh." He sucked his cheeks in, biting gently. His axe-butt rested upon the stone walkway, and he folded his hands atop the well-seasoned eye. Metal glinted, etched with frost. "What do you think, K'ai?"

Finally, he was not speaking to me as if I were one of his fat white countrywomen. "I think I will wait until he is at the Keep."

"At the Keep?" Now he glanced at me, bloodshot blue eyes narrowed afresh. He was not sleeping well, or he was finding solace in an ale-tankard each night. From the smell, I judged it to be the latter.

"There, there, and there." I pointed each time to likely avenues of approach, my half-gloves already caked with ice. The wind intensified, and even the warming breath only kept the worst of the chill at bay. "It is only a matter of time, and they will grow desperate if they fire all their shelter. Dunkast must keep control of them. Or regain control, soon." I folded my arms, awkward in their bundling. "The walls are breached, the East Gate is forced, but his men have not drawn close enough yet for me to make a difference. So, I wait."

"K'ai…" It was clearly not what he had expected me to say.

I cared little. "Tonight I shall take to the rooftops, and make his forces fear for their lives." *Much as the Danhai would.* "But that is only a prelude. He will have to enter the city proper, in order to keep control of his forces and their pillage."

Redfist now watched me sidelong. The very end of his axe-hilt touched the ground and made a slight noise, grinding in dirt and slush. "And then?"

Why, in the name of the Moon, was he asking? Did he merely wish to hear me say it? I longed for Darik's silence instead of Redfist's clumsy company. "Then I will find where he is laying his curséd head, slip inside the building, and slide a knife between his ribs." *I have done such things before.* "And take his head as well, for one cannot be too certain, with witchery like this. There are stories of the Pensari—"

"*Assassinate* him?"

I refrained from pointing out, *again*, that Dunkast did not seem inclined to duel honorably, and my plan at least had some chance of success. "Do you have a better proposal, Rainak Redfist? One which may see us all through this alive?"

"I wish to meet him in the open—"

"Oh, yes, because that plan worked *so well* before." I indicated the burning with a thrust of my chin. "Do you think he has any *intention* of facing you honorably, or did when he came into Kalburn Keep? If you do, you are the fool I never thought you."

"Ye did not think I was a fool?"

I may have to revise my belief. "Not a great one, no."

"Ye have a sharp tongue, K'ai." As if he was taken

aback. He lifted his axe a little, thocked the butt-end against stone to punctuate the sentence.

Well, my tongue had not been *blunt* since well before he happened along in Hain; he could not expect that to change. "Necessary, to pierce a collection of stubborn skulls." I exhaled sharply, and was surprised when my breath did not immediately turn to ice and fall tinkling to the ground. "I shall ask your Needleslay to draw me a map or two of her city. Then I shall go hunting."

"K'ai—"

"What, Redfist?" I half-turned, faced him squarely. "You do not wish my aid? You will call me dishonorable? I am *far* better than that thing outside the walls, and you would do well to remember, and treat me, as such. I will do as I must to gain us all passage through this swamp." Harsher words trembled upon my tongue, halted only by the cold and the fact that I was heartily sick of this entire country as well as every half-baked idiot who had attached themselves to me.

Consequently, I was almost certain I would say something that would force him to attempt to throw me from the battlements.

"Ye are not meant for the Highlands, K'ai." He shook his great bushy head. "In the South, they may knife each other in bed, or send assassins, but we are Kroth's children here."

"Dunkast has *already* sent assassins, Redfist!" The force of my cry almost pushed me back upon my heels and fell away into the grasp of the wind. Did he truly not understand? What went on inside his skull if not a constant whirling of stones attempting to make a grind so fine the resultant meal would feed, clothe, and protect our troupe? "What do you think those two Ferulaine in Karnagh were? Or the Black Brother here in Kalburn, do you think that latter gift sent for *you*?" The dart went home. His eyes widened, and I could have struck him, did I wish to take my hands from their slightly warmer homes under my elbows. "You did not think of that? Of *why* Dunkast would send such a thing, before word could have reached him you were sitting at sup in Emrath's Great Hall, witchery or no?" I shook my head, wonderingly. "You *are* a fool. And you will not only achieve your own death but Emrath Needleslay's, too."

I turned upon my heel and strode away, and for a few moments I was warm despite the wind. Mother's *tits*, had he not thought any of this through? Did he have only their congealed milk *marag* in his skull? I decided, only a few paces away, that not only was Rainak Redfist a fool, but it was also my duty to save him from his great lumpen self.

It was, after all, the only way to save us all.

I meant to find Emrath Needleslay and make some manner of cause with her, but instead, as I plunged back into the Keep's relative warmth, I was found instead.

By Gavridar Janaire.

AID, NO AID

THE WIND FELL OFF; I stamped upon the slippery stone stairs to clear my boots. Of course she could find me with little trouble, such things are easy for a trained *adai*. Looking up, her hip against a wooden casement covering an arrow-slit, her lengthening braids wrapped winter-wise around her head and her soft, pretty face solemn, she was a garden-statue. The casement rattled as sky's-breath clawed at its bolts, and Janaire studied me for a long moment before speaking.

"Anjalismir." My clan-name, formally accented, almost palpable ice along its edges. Her needle had been at work among the folds of her great fur-lined cloak, refining the shape. It had probably been plied upon Atyarik's clothes, too.

To add to my faults, I was no seamstress—I may, of course, repair a jerkin or trews if I must. But a sellsword prefers to hire such work done, all the better to leave time for dicing and knifeplay, not to mention sword practice, and sleeping. Or drinking, if I could find enough mead in the storerooms to blunt my head. The idea was marvelously attractive, though the danger of being sotted while an entire army invades will make even a seasoned sellsword blanch.

"Gavridar," I replied, just as stiffly. But I took care to make my inflection as respectful as possible. "If you wish to slap me, very well, I shall stay still for it." It was, I told myself, only fair. If I could say there was no satisfaction in striking her, I would not have offered.

She shook her head. Her ear-drops, fine silver and dark-red stones, swung. She and Emrath Needleslay could decorate themselves thus; there was no risk of the gems being torn from her head during battle. "Perhaps later. Your *s'tarei* fears your temper."

"So he sent you to sweeten it?" It stung me, briefly. Then again, D'ri had reason to be wary. I could not be the *adai* he wanted, the twin all *s'tarei* were raised to expect, and that disappointment was all the more deep, I suspected, because he would not give it voice. I wondered if I should speak to her in tradetongue, simply to drive my point home.

"That seems to be my task." Her mantle sleeves, deep-folded and prettily shaped, fell at exactly the right angle on either side. Faint light striped her face from the casement's gaps. "I hold little belief it can be done."

You would not be the first to despair of such a thing. I sought levity, and tried a crooked, cheek-sore smile. "Then you are wise for your age."

Her somberness did not crack. She regarded me with large, liquid, beautiful eyes. "And you foolish for yours. The witching-gem is *dangerous*. My *s'tarei* and yours are in accord: it would be best to leave this place."

"You should have thought to flee *before* the walls of this very keep were sieged, then." My own eyes were too light, a golden gaze that had earned me trouble along the Rim. It was merely another flaw, one of the many. "I know Gavrin has no sense, and Diyan even less, but *you*, Yada'Adais." The honorific did not choke me; she had earned it with her patience. I knew I was not the best of students, but I could call flame now and keep the borders of my mind inviolate. "You were to keep them in Antai for the winter, where I would not have to worry. Now how am I to bring you all through this mess?" I used the word for a tangle of bramble that could be avoided if one had simply looked ahead, each syllable accented high and sharp.

"The little one took fright, and hied himself off after you alone." Janaire's shoulders went back and her chin came up. She did not look conscious of having the lower ground in this particular battle. She did not even look *cold*, but perhaps her grasp of the warming breath was greater than mine. "Gavrin did not wish to come, nor did I wish him to, but he was the one who had...oh, it is *useless* explaining to you. You will not listen."

I could have pointed out that I *would* listen, I simply did not care what excuse was offered. She, of all of them, should have had the sense to stay in safety, and Atyarik would do so at her bidding. A fully trained *adai* and *s'tarei* could have kept a wayward lutebanger and a Vulfentown wharf-rat inside the city, I was certain of that much. "And you did not drag Diyan back to Antai? Why not?"

"Well, we had already started. And I...I feared you would meet some mishap, and that surely it were better for us to face it together than apart." Her chin set stubbornly, I almost felt it in my own body, like a *s'tarei*'s pain. "It is impolite for you to treat those who wish to aid you so harshly."

My patience slipped a fraction. "If *aid* was what

you could offer, I would not! A child, a lutebanger, a half-grown G'mai girl and a *s'tarei* unconcerned with anything but keeping *her* skin whole—what would *aid* me would be a full division of regulars, or even a cadre of experienced thieves." *And, while I am dreaming, a few assassins and a Pesh fire-slinger or two might not be amiss.* My hands were fists, and my frustration trembled at the edge of my grasp. "How am I to protect you all, if you will not stay where I place you?" And now, how I would keep my little troupe whole when—not *if*, I was beginning to think, but *when*— the Keep fell?

"Where you place us, Anjalismir?" She almost blanched, and there were shadows under her pretty eyes. The mark on her cheek had faded completely, but battle-shock and a strike to bring you forth from its clutches are neither restful nor pleasant. "Like toys."

"Like *those I care for*!" I bellowed like a Shainakh serjeant taking new recruits to task, like one Antai fishmonger fighting another for stall space, like a drunken sellsword.

It did not seem to affect her. She merely turned thoughtful, staring up at me. Her hands fell loosely to her sides, no longer laced before her belly. "Ah. I see."

No. You do not. "I cannot bear the thought of harm coming to you." Each word was a knife, and I flung them at her. "I undertook to protect you all, but now there is an *entire army* at the walls, and you are no help, Gavridar Janaire. Would that I had sent you back to G'maihallan." The urge to shout again rasped at my throat, and every muscle on me knotted itself. There was no battle here, I reminded myself. But dear gods, I longed to strike something, anything, to relieve this awful pressure.

"Oh, aye. Would that you had, princess." The term

for an Heir's *adai* was just as sharply accented as my own speech. Janaire half-turned, presenting me with her perfect profile. "But we are here now, and if *you* do not wish our aid, perhaps there are others who do." With that, she sailed away down the stairs, a graceful ghost whispering over rude-carved Skaialan stone, and I considered driving my fist into the stone wall.

I did not, but only because it was too cold. And because soon, very soon, I—and both fists—would be needed elsewhere.

BEFORE A NIGHT PATROL

WINTER in the Highlands means night comes swift, early, and cold. Darkness drops from an iron-grey sky like a hen brooding over eggfruit, and with it and snow comes the sky-breathing they call *faure-gauithhe* or, if they are irreligious, *Kroth's wind*. The latter term holds a play upon their term for a certain bodily function, much as the phrase for dropping a lamp into an ill-ventilated privy does in Shainakh. Some of the *truly* foul-mouthed among them have another term, centering on a certain female cavity of their goddess of childbirth and illness, and I heard the latter more than once during the siege of Kalburn Keep. On that first night, though, in the kitchens, there was no bellowing, no boasting, and no servants scrubbing. Emrath Needleslay lifted her skirts free of the floor-rushes and watched while I prepared myself for a night patrol.

How far was I from the Danhai plains? I could count the horse-steps during a day's travel like the barbarians there did. I could even, did I have the head for it, count the Shainak *ells* or the Hain *li*, or the Freetown *milus* or the Pesh *granik*, all different divisions of how far one could travel in a quarter-candlemark on their respective roads. Except a Shainakh *ell* was a measure of grain-ground too, and there was also the Freetown *banus*, how far a ratbird could fly in a tenth of a candlemark.

The Needleslay's nose wrinkled at some of the preparations. "I cannae promise ye any help."

At least there was no shortage of cooking-fat yet, or soot. "Good," I said, smearing a dollop of rancid grease across my cheeks, then rubbing fat-mixed chimney-crumb over it. There was not even the prospect of a bath afterward to cleanse myself, just the oil and the *skauna*. When I returned to civilization—*if* I did—I would drown myself in baths thrice daily for a week. It was a pleasant thought. "Anyone your size would merely get in the way." I glanced at D'ri, changing to G'mai. "Darik, are you certain you wish to—"

"Why must you ask?" Darik, grim-faced, spread the foul mixture on his own cheekbones. It made him look fierce, bringing out the fey glitter in his dark gaze and accenting the planes of his Dragaemir-strong face. "Atyarik wished to come night-hunting as well."

Now *that* was an uncomfortable prospect. "Unless he's forgiven me for striking Janaire, I think it unwise."

"He was…unhappy." It was all D'ri would say of the matter. Twin *dotani* hilts over his shoulders, a bow with its string treated for the cold, a quiver of black-fletched arrows—he was skilled at coney-hunting, my *s'tarei*. Tonight there would be different prey. "But he had to admit it worked."

A laugh caught at my throat—the sharp, half-swallowed chuckle I'd heard too many times before on the Plains before a battle or ambush. I had thought to leave the mud, and the blood, and the tribes behind. How many of the irregulars I served with were still alive?

Were the plains pursuing *them*, too? What would Ammerdahl Rikyat say of *this*?

Probably just the usual. *Tie down the jangles, blacken your blades, and let us be done with it.* His voice drifted in memory-halls, a thin cricket-whisper.

My left hand jumped, made an *avert* sign. Ill-luck, to hear the dead before a night patrol.

"Ye do not have enough arrows." Emrath's knuckles whitened. Not as calm as she liked to appear, the Lady of Kalburn nevertheless stayed to watch our preparations. Very likely she imagined we would be dead before sunrise, and wished our shades not to return crying of ill-treatment by our hostess.

"We do not need many tonight." I examined the blacking upon my largest knife. The Moon was in her waning half, there would be little but torchlight to wring a betraying gleam from metal or eye-white. "Only enough to frighten."

"I would speak with thee." The lady of Kalburn cast a nervous glance at Darik. "Alone."

Now is not the time. I shrugged. Perhaps she wished to bless me before battle. "Whatever you have to say to me, my *s'tarei* may hear." I glanced at D'ri, but his head was down as he ran his fingers over the arrows, brushing the fletching and making certain he knew where each individual, heavy-headed or fine, had settled.

Emrath glanced at him too, but forged onward. "It concerns Rainak." Another nervous look, this time at me; her blue-stone ear-drops swayed. A fine dewing on her forehead—well, she had every right to be nervous. Her city was under siege and her husband was a ravening sorcerer with a witched Pensari gem.

"Does it?" I slid the knife into its home, careful

not to disturb the blacking. "How long have you been working against Dunkast?" It was an easy guess. Oh, Corran Ninefinger had only been a stalking-goat for the Ferulaine; the evidence for Emrath's plans lay elsewhere, in Dunkast sending men to watch Karnagh's inns and Kalburn's trade-routes, and the Black Brother entering her Great Hall. None of her *tain* seemed surprised by Dunkast's attack—certainly they thought him mad, and dangerous, but they were not taken completely unaware.

She was a weaver, the lady of Kalburn, and that craft requires patience. And planning.

"Since he destroyed his own adopted clan, put Rainak in chains, and forced marriage upon me." Grey eyes, wary and worried in equal measure, met mine. She dropped her fine blue skirts and pushed her shoulders back, facing me as if we stood upon a dueling-ground. "Do ye love him?"

What? I tried to replay the sentence inside my head, and found my Skaialan lacking. "What?"

"Rainak. Do ye *love* him?" She cast yet another nervous glance at Darik, who stopped his own preparations, returning her gaze with no little astonishment.

I thought perhaps I had misheard her Skaialan again. "Redfist is my friend," I said, carefully. "What do you ask me, Emrath Needleslay?" It was strange to put a kin-name before a given-name, but everything in the Highlands was backward.

"I ask if ye wish him for yerself, Lady Gemerh." Brittle and formal, and now her sly looks at Darik made a mad manner of sense. Her hem draggled in dirty rushes and spent sweetstraw. "We were contracted, the Conniahgt Crae's son and I. Then Dunkast made his own clan, and since then, all has been for naught."

"Kaia?" Darik, perplexed, paused in the act of slinging his quiver. "What does she ask you?"

"I…" For a moment, none of the languages I knew seemed fit to suffice. "I think…oh." I chose Skaialan, and hoped I could make myself understood. "I have no marriage-interest in Redfist, Lady Needleslay." I pointed at D'ri, whose bafflement now deepened. "*That*, as you Skaialan term it, is my husband."

"Do yer kind take more than one?" She smoothed her skirts, a quick, habitual, soothing motion. Perhaps that is how a woman who wears such things readies herself for battle. "I do not know much of the Blest."

I struggled with the urge to laugh. I could explain that the Hain contract group marriages, and so do many in the Freetowns among the merchant clans; Pesh men take several wives or concubines if they can afford them, and two or three shield-husbands if their god moves them to that affection. In Antai there are trade-marriages and adoptions to strengthen the great merchant houses, and in Shainakh a woman might marry her husband's brother to get heirs if said husband proves impotent…but I did not think now the time for a discussion of the many forms cohabitation or affection might take. Even among the G'mai there are terms for affection between two *s'tarei*, or two *adai* who wish to share more than polite regard or even deep friendship.

Love should never be wasted.

"D'ri is my *s'tarei*," I said, firmly. "There is, and will only ever *be*, only one. Redfist is my *friend*. I hold no, er, wish for him to be as a Skaialan marries." Clumsy, but what I knew of their language was not meant for this manner of discussion.

"I have seen the way he looks at ye." Emrath, unsatisfied, leaned forward, and were she a sellsword I would think her close to drawing a blade. "I have *seen* it."

What, did she think he wished to lie with me? The very idea was laughable, even if I would consent to let him there was still the matter of his bulk crushing any woman not his size. "He looks upon me as a strange pet that has a human tongue. If there is one he would take as twin—I mean, *wife*, Needleslay, I believe it is you." It cost me nothing to say it, and I could even believe it true. After all, the first thing he had done was kiss her, and his feelings on her 'marriage' were obviously anything but calm.

She nodded, her shoulders sinking. Her cheeks had reddened, perhaps with embarrassment.

"What does she ask you?" Darik was interested, now, and wished an explanation in G'mai instead of tradetongue. At least he appeared just as baffled as I.

"She asked me if Redfist was my *s'tarei*. Or if I wished him as such." I could not help it, a short laugh boiled free. I sobered almost instantly, though—those who laugh too much before a night patrol will weep after. My hands moved of their own accord, stowing knives, making certain of no betraying clink or clank. I doubted we would be heard over the wind, but you could never tell when moving air would carry the sound of metal meeting upon its back far enough to make mischief.

"Ah." His brow knit. Darik bounced on his toes a few times, to make certain all his own gear was not likely to rattle and to test his quiver's weight. "Well?"

I halted, and regarded him across a great block of wooden table, now scattered with implements and dark cloth to wind around hilt, head, or wrists. "Well, *what?*"

"Do you wish for him?" He resettled his quiver, ran his fingers over the fletchings again. There was no term in G'mai for such a thing, instead, he used the phrase for a child's longing to have a toy. "I have wondered."

"Mother *Moon*, no." My jaw threatened to drop to my chest. "He is a great red brainless lump, D'ri, and I have a *s'tarei*." I stared at him, frankly astonished. "Why, in the name of every god, would *you* ask me this?"

He shrugged, bouncing on his toes twice again, seeing how the straps settled. Satisfied, he dropped his weight into his heels, and finished tidying the table, his hands moving sure and graceful among the detritus of preparation. "I have wondered. I shall wait for you outside."

He finished, turned on his heel, and strode for the door with nary a sound. I stared at his weapons-laden back; Emrath Needleslay eyed me with a great deal of bright interest. "So he saw it too," she remarked. "How did *you* not?"

"There was nothing to see." If we were dueling, I decided it was time to stop parrying and make a cut or two of my own. "You did not think Redfist would be able to call the Clans, did you."

"Oh, I did. Kroth love that big red bastard, I knew he was fine enough to strike the Anvil." She rubbed at her eyes, delicately massaging the skin. "We planned to rise against the Ferulaine in spring after the mud and planting had passed, and Ninefinger was to tell Rainak as much."

Ah. That answered more than one question, and made sense besides. "You should not have trusted him."

"He was part of Redfist's *tain*." Emrath glared at me, but there was little heat to it. "And what do ye know of who to trust in the Highlands, lady Gemerh?"

Now she was formal. It was an unexpected relief. "Simple. I treat you *all* as if you mean to kill Redfist, or me." I gave her my dueling-smile, wide, bright, and unsettling, driving her back a step as her hem brushed aside rushes and straw. "Go to bed, Needleslay, and sleep well. Tonight death will walk in your city, and take the Ferulaine's men."

I left her in that under-kitchen, and perhaps I should not have been so dismissive. We were, after all, depending on her orders to let us back *into* the Keep after our night's work.

BELOW THE RIDGELINE

THE SKAIALAN SING of the Breaking of Kalburn, how the Needleslay's faithful *tain* put up flaming barricades and made the bastard clans fight for each curve in the cobbled streets, each corner, each vantage point. They were quick and canny, the Needlelslay's men, and supplemented by Jorak Blacknose and his fellows, for Highland bards have a witchery all their own. A true Skaialan bard may exhort men to fight with capacity beyond mere flesh, or sing a song that drags at their opponents, chaining limbs and muddying the will. Precious few things are proof against the wall of sound a Skaialan harper may raise from a throat trained in their old ways. I heard long after that the test for those who wish to be called *bard* is to swallow molten lead, and I more than halfway believe it.

When night came, however, both sides retreated to what shelter they could find. The darkness was full of ice, and howling, and those sent on watch at the barricades or in high windows shiver and curse their luck, relieved every quarter-candlemark and carried inside half-frozen.

The Skaialan do not sing of Kalburn at night. It is

as well, for they know nothing, those giants, of what we truly accomplished, my *s'tarei* and me.

Steep-pitched, icy roofs, far colder than any winter thiefwalk in Antai or Shaitush or any of the great Hain cities upon the Rim. The trick is to stay below the ridgeline, to rob any follower or opponent of your silhouette, and to, as far as you can, cut *across* the slope instead of climbing or descending it. It is, I will not deny, easier when you have a *s'tarei* whose step is light, and a breath of Power or two to help your boots stick. What also helped were the maps Emrath had let me study, each quarter of the Old City drawn in painstaking detail. They were for tax purposes, those great sheets of pounded rag-paper, but for those six nights of the Great Siege of Kalburn while the wind brought fresh cargoes of snow and keened at every edge, while those on guard were dragged inside to be revived with ale and vigorous slapping, they were my faithful friends. For a long time after I could close my eyes and trace routes across their inked spaces, flashes filling internal vision—a particular crumbling roof that held us while D'ri, anchored by my grip upon the back of his jacket, leaned far out to send an arrow into a Ferulaine watchman's throat; an alley we slithered into to dart across a narrow, filth-crusted street and through a shattered door, a knife blooming in a guard's throat and the squad of Skaialan bravos inside dying as they huddled in their furs or struggled out of cold-induced nightmares, my foot flicking out to tip a brazier's cargo of burning blackrock onto one who began to scream as his oily bed-hides turned to flame-blossoms; the long sweep along one side of the Great Market of Kalburn, any stalls that could not be dragged away lashed tightly together, its great open expanse lit with flickering bonfires and D'ri choosing targets one, two, three by their leaping light.

No, they do not truly sing of Kalburn's siege at night. Instead, they sing of how Kroth's anger sent shadows and ghosts among the Ferulaine, sowing death where they willed. By the third dawn, when D'ri and I climbed hand-over-hand up a knotted rope and gained the safety of a keep window-casement left unlocked for us, spilling into the room beyond with grateful groans, there had already been much of it, and much confusion to harvest.

By the fourth, the inhabitants of the Old City had begun to take matters into their own hands as well. By day, the Ferulaine swaggered almost up to the walls of the Keep. By night, however, by ones and twos, they disappeared. Bodies thumped into the street. They began to avoid guard duty, and that made it easier to slip about unseen *and* to take them in larger batches—for example, stopping a chimney to smoke them into the street where they could be picked off almost at will.

I had learned well the lessons of the Plains. A few Danhai could turn an entire battalion of Shainakh regulars into nerve-strung idiots jumping at every sibilant breath through the choygrass. It does not take much to unsettle your opponent, if you have somewhere to hide during the day. All fear the things which walk at night, even hardened sellswords.

But Dunkast stayed outside the Old City. There were houses along the East Wall he had kept them from firing, and there he crouched. Eventually he would have to come into the city, and then I would have him, I could almost *taste* it.

The sixth night began well enough, with D'ri and I running further afield than we had yet dared past the Great Market and into a quarter of taverns, outdoor privies, and covered *torkascruagh* pens, their inhabitants in normal times let loose at the end of the short winter days to clean the Great Market's floor of offal, dropped things, and any other detritus. I had some idea of seeing if D'ri's ability to coax the splithoof beasts would lure them into some manner of insurrection as well.

Once, the Danhai had used a grassfire to drive a herd of wild horses through an irregulars' camp, and had a fine time hunting the survivors. I know, for I was one of them. Now I wondered what they felt, those high-crested tribesfolk, and my decision to sign with the irregulars to avoid dueling the father of the young man who had attempted to cage me seemed a matter of saving one life by killing many elsewhere.

Much later, I found out the father had died of fever while I was in the mud and blood and stink of the third great Danhai offensive. How could I have known?

You should have, Kaia. Each time I thought upon the matter, the same answer rose. *You should have known better.*

D'ri halted, his knees going loose, and for a moment I thought the cold had struck him down. But no, it was merely the instinct of a thief on a rooftop, stopping without making noise or sending a loose tile plunging. He would have made a fine thief, my *s'tarei*.

I almost plowed into him, halted just in time, and went into a crouch—the one instinct he had *not* learned yet, and it almost killed us both. I still do not know what made my foot flick out, catching him behind the knee. It could not have been the whistle of a bolt overhead, for the sound does not travel as swiftly in the confines of an ice-rimed street. Out upon the Plains, you may sometimes hear the missile before it reaches you if the wind is right, but in city-hunting?

No. Instinct saved us both—or Power, whispering in my ear.

My *s'tarei* went down hard, the crossbow quarrel cleaving air where his skull had been a moment before, and tumbled for the edge of the roof.

Dunkast, tiring of the siege, had sent his Black Brothers into Kalburn to do a little night-hunting of their own.

COB-COLORED MARE

DARIK DID NOT PLUMMET three floors to the cobbles, only because I made fish-lunging, wrenching lunge and ended up sideways, bleeding momentum with thrashing arms and legs, scraping over icy tiles and slowing us both *just* enough. Another bolt whistled past, curving sharply to crunch into the roof, plowing sharp tile-chips in a deadly spray. I rolled free of Darik's limbs, my entire body singing with the metallic clarity of battle, and gained my feet with a lunge that threatened to tear something in my left side. Ran along the edge of the roof, hearing the *thunk-thuk-thuk* of crossbows singing, giving them a clear target so my *s'tarei* had time to gain his wits and his balance. Chips flew, and men yelled in Skaialan.

Something's wrong. How had they known we were atop that particular roof? Were their eyes that keen? Had a stray gleam given us away—

"*Kaia!*" Darik, behind me.

A sharp burst of yellow irritation filled my mouth with bitterness. I was drawing the bastards' bolts so he could unlimber his bow, why was he *yelling*? I skidded to a stop, throwing my top half back, knees scraping painfully even through the reinforced patches on my trews as a blade whistled overhead. My left hand blurred for my largest knife; my right had already leapt for my *dotani* and halted, diving instead for my middle-knife, one filed for throwing.

My opponent was a hulking shadow, scrambling sideways with eerie, ungainly grace. My right hand smacked down, half-gloved fist braced by knifehilt, giving me another point of contact with the roof as my left knee jumped up. If I could hook his knee with my left foot and *twist*, my largest knife could strike, flickering just-so into his thigh and hopefully opening the artery.

I did not get the chance. He was too fast, and his boot slammed into my belly. Breath and sense both left me for a weightless moment, shocked lungs struggling to function; I slid sideways down the tiles, my head striking painfully and my shoulder giving a brief popping flare of hot pain as I tried to drive my right-hand knife *down*. It screeched along tiles, digging through ice, and the crossbows were silent now.

They had done their work.

A creeping, deadly, soft stickiness warred with the cold. I retched, harshly, and the shadow was above me again. It was a Black Brother, full of that queer inhuman looseness in all the joints, and I realized it was too dark not because the Moon was low and waning but because a bruise of clotted Power hung around the thing that had once been a man.

That was why the foul gloves are doubly dangerous to *adai*, much as an infected boil is dangerous to an otherwise healthy body. If lanced, there is a chance the rest of the body will recover, but if it bursts inward, the woundrot races through internal pathways and even a many-skilled Clau or Haiian healer cannot save you. The pus from such swellings reeks of corpsebreath, and can spread woundrot to any wounded bedmate as well.

An *adai*, born exquisitely sensitive to Power and with that sensitivity nurtured since childhood, could easily be mazed by the unphysical stench and their unholy speed. As it was, *I* was bred, but not sensitive. A lifetime spent denying my own Power with a child's intensity was enough to insulate me.

Or so I had thought, when I considered meeting another Black Brother; I had not been allowed to strike the one in Kalburn's Great Hall. This one had a sword, straight and heavy—not the best for rooftop work, with uncertain footing and a small target. But he did not need to be quick when his prey sprawled witless, shaking her braids, trying to clear her skull and force her lungs to work properly again. He only needed to be thorough, and lift his bright length of killing metal high. Of course the crossbow-wielders would either be reloading, or know that an un-blacked blade was one of their own.

Move, Kaia. MOVE!

I could have rolled for the edge; the drop at *this* end of the roof might only break a few bones if I was lucky. Instead, I flung my left shoulder up, lungs still burning, my belly a white-hot mass of pain.

I have been kicked in the stomach before, and by an ill-tempered Shainakh army mare. There is a story why they began calling me *kaahai* in the irregulars, for I got up after that cob-colored horse threw me across the picket line, tossed a rope bridle over her head, and took her for a bone-rattling, bucking, wild gallop across the autumn heat of the Plains just before the rains arrived to make hip-deep mud everywhere, riding until she learned my stubbornness outmatched hers.

She was the best horse I'd ever taken into battle,

mean-tempered and diabolically intelligent, and the only thing I regretted was not naming her before the battle that put a crossbow bolt in both her chest and Ammerdahl Rikyat's back.

You shall not die, Ammerdahl Rikyat. You owe me at dice. Perhaps my luck had run out.

I could not stab the foul glove's thigh, but my left hand shot out, blade reversed along my forearm, and caught his naked shin, grinding on bone after the thin skin and the long straplike anterior muscle parted. Which might have been enough to throw him off, but I curled around myself, wrapping around his right ankle too. My blade overshot, breaking free of shinbone and catching bootleather, then hooked back and bit deeply into his other calf.

Let us see how well you dance now, friend.

Freezing air filled my lungs again, and Darik *arrived*. Rattle of tiles, he launched himself, and his own boots, spark-crackling with Power, thudded into the Brother's side. The big Skaialan, still a mere shadow to me, thumped aside, joints gone doll-loose, and rolled for the edge, his huge booted toe grabbing the inside of my elbow and almost taking my largest knife, my arm, and the rest of me with him.

Clatter of metal hitting tile, a vise about my left wrist, a hoarse shout of effort. I wrenched my knife free and the Brother, tumbling like a mass of wet laundry, spilled over the edge and into empty air.

I did not wait for the sound of body striking cobbles, a vicious curse hissing through my teeth as I attempted to surge up and my belly spasmed again, breath and sense both threatening to leave me until I ceased my rooftop-running ways.

"Kaia!" D'ri did not yell, but the word still carried. I heard another low, deadly sound and went limp, his hand around my wrist biting as I pulled him the only possible direction—over and on top of me, hoping I would not stab him with either blade. He had dropped his left-hand *dotani* to catch me, and the roof's ridgeline behind him boiled with large, ungainly, loose-limbed shapes.

How many of those foul abominations did the cursed Ferulaine *have*? *Too many* was the answer, and the only thing in our favor was the crossbows' silence for fear of hitting their own. It was a well-laid trap—how many others had Dunkast set across Kalburn?

One trap is too many, Kaia, when you have sprung it unaware. Copper laid against the back of my tongue. Darik landed on me, driving all my breath out once more.

If I ever managed to breathe again, I would visit a temple and make an offering, I decided. Any god would do, the first one I saw a temple for, even Kroth the head-god of this awful place. It wouldn't hurt; the Moon, though jealous of Her children, would certainly understand.

"*Hai!*" someone yelled, a familiar cry from a gruff throat. It was a *s'tarei*'s practice-yell when a strike landed, and sudden bright-orange blossoms cast crazy, dappling shadows. A low *wump* was clothing igniting, and a Black Brother, suddenly aflame, began to scream in a queer, high, keening voice like a hurt child.

A massive noise rent the night below and Darik surged upwards, finding his balance and lunging across me to scoop up his fallen *dotani*. Then he was off, almost bent double against the slope of the ridgeline, running to aid Tyaanismir Atyarik, who was moving with all a *s'tarei*'s speed and grace, stabbing the burning Black Brother, and screamed his defiance again.

CLASH-SLITHER MUSIC

I MADE it to hands and knees, cough-choking, and the impossible happened. A shadow swelled next to me, and I almost planted my right-hand knife in Janaire's throat. She grabbed my shoulders, a great furred hood falling back from her high-braided hair, and her soft face was the Moon's in darkness, beautiful and serene. She glanced over her shoulder, Power sparked, and she jabbed a pair of fingers at another Black Brother, who began screaming in that same, high, childlike voice as he beat at the flames suddenly blooming from his rancid clothing. D'ri hit him, *dotanii* whirling in solid arcs, and I hissed another curse.

The *idiots*. Now they were lit for the crossbows.

But the half-dozen crossbows below did not speak, for Jorak Blacknose, his throat fortified with no little Skaialan bitter, foul-smelling ale, had dealt with *them*, and in fine fashion too. He'd sung a mad-dening-song to the penned *torkascruagh* and sent no few of them over the slippery, heaving cobbles right into the knot of bowmen. It stank of a battlefield be-low, and above there was flame and the spectacle of two *s'tarei*, both masters of their trade, dueling giants who burst into flame as Janaire made one hoarse sound of effort after another.

It was a fine battle, but it was not *quiet*. I dragged in one breath after another, promptly forgetting my offering-vow like all good sellswords granted a few more moments of survival, and gathered my legs under me. Below, Jorak Blacknose hefted himself onto the slippery, heaving back of a maddened, shaggy black *torkascruagh*, wheeling the beast's head around by the simple expedient of leaning forward to grab its ears. He gave another musical cry, and the beasts lowed, stamping, and wheeled, following him like a flock of woolcoats and their bellwether.

Janaire made another low sound of effort. Calling flame is no easy task in the midst of a battle, but she held to her work with grim determination. I shoved my right-hand knife into its home, found my legs would indeed carry me, and pushed myself up, drawing my *dotani*.

I meant to charge into the fray, but Janaire grabbed my left knee, her fingers sinking in with surprising strength. Her other hand jabbed out again, fingers fluttering, and I *felt* her pulling at Power, shaping it to her will, the effort stinging her eyes with salt sweat and dampening her skin under layers of cloth and fur. Her face was incandescent, and a pang went through me before I tore my knee from her grasp and surged forward.

I was more use with a blade than with Power, and well I knew it.

The last Black Brother gurgled, D'ri's blade blurring to open his throat, the other blade reversed to bite even more deeply. They were taking the heads, to be safe. Arterial spray blossomed and stinking smoke rose in veils. Darik cried aloud, a *s'tarei*'s battle-madness filling him with clear red rage.

Or was it mine? I could not tell. Steel met steel, clash-slither music.

I snapped a glance at the street. At the near end, torchlight ran and sputtered. The alarum was well and truly raised; now it was a footrace. We would need swiftness and cunning to avoid the net.

I could not worry for the Skaialan bard; if I managed to gain safety for the other G'mai, it would have to be good enough. I would have liked to know how they followed me, but that could wait. There was one Black Brother left. I hurtled past Atyarik, *dotani* held low for the sweep, main knife reversed along my left forearm to ward off the descent—not of his axeblade, for that might have broken my arm or cut me too deeply to stanch. No, my speed—even winded and tender-bellied, struggling in layers of heat-conserving cloth and fur—was enough, again, and I took the strike of the axe-handle along the flat of the blade as my *dotani* swept in, my right hip popping out to provide leverage for the twist, the blade punching deep. His other hand was high, he bore two single-axes, not one of the massive double monsters.

I took the only move I could. Falling back, twisting in midair, letting the slope to my back pull me down and away while my *dotani* whipped through his abdomen and a steaming lump of viscera spilled free, spattering noisome fluid in a wide spray. The twist saved me from being bathed, and Atyarik's left-hand *dotani* whirled in, biting deep in the Skaialan's neck. It takes some doing to sever a head, and chipping your blade on the cervical vertebrae is unpleasant at best.

But a *dotani* in the hands of one trained by G'mai warmasters can find the spaces *between* bone, and whisper through like a lover at a keyhole. Or so tis said, and should you ever see a *s'tarei* fight, you will see it is truth.

"Kaia!" Darik's hand on the back of my jacket. He hauled me away, my foot turned on a tile, and we almost slid down the roof *again* and fell to the cobbles.

The steam-smoking bodies lay scattered-strewn. Was the structure below empty? If not, were they listening to a pitched battle overhead as they huddled in cold darkness, or near a low fire?

Darik set his heels, halting us, and dragged me upright. "Are you hurt? *Are* you?"

I will feel this in the morn, should we live that long. "No," I snapped, and glanced over the bodies. The night had taken on its usual darkness, without the creeping ink of the foul gloves. My ribs heaved. "Is that all of them?"

"Tis." Atyarik slid past us, his boots sticking with Power and authority, and offered Janaire his hand. "Are you well, *adai'mi?*"

"My head," Janaire said faintly, her G'mai a whisper. "Ugh. I shall be well enough."

"You should *not* have attacked him." Darik let go of my jacket, and I whipped effluvia from my *dotani*. "They are *dangerous*, Kaia!"

"I *know!*" I strode to the nearest body, wiped my blade on still-smoking clothing. Fingers twitched, and the thing moved slightly against the tiles, nerve-death pulling blindly at muscle-strings. My gorge rose, pointlessly; I quelled it. My belly was full of hot coals. "I was not offering him a lovesong, D'ri. Come, we'd best be gone. There will be more."

His hand shot out, closed around my upper arm. He pulled, all but dragging me away from the corpse. "Are you not *listening?* You could have been hurt, Kaia. You could have—"

"I am *not*, and we must move." I wished to enquire

just how Janaire and Atyarik had followed us, but that could wait. *Everything* could wait until I had all three of them tucked safely into Kalburn Keep. "We have announced our presence to the entire city, and if there are more of the foul gloves, they are already on their way. What of Blacknose?"

"What of—" His expression changed; even in that half-light, I could see it. A soft suspicion tiptoed through the fog of battle-nerves, quivering muscle pain, and my bruised ribs. I could not get enough air in, now that the battle was done.

I doubted I would ever be able to again.

So I simply bent my knees, tested the grip of my bootsoles, surveyed the rooftops around us, and hoped we were not already caught. "Come. And for the love of the Moon, try to keep up."

BLOOD-TINGED TICKLE

WE WERE NOT CAUGHT. Not right away, at least, and not completely.

I remember little of that gallop across the roofs of Kalburn's Old City, hampered by my inability to catch my breath and the slowness of two G'mai who, though fit and trained, were *not* schooled in the trick of moving across rooftops. I had no air to ask them how or why, I simply set a punishing pace and racked my head-meat to take us on a long looping path back to the Keep. There was the difference between the maps and the rooftop terrain, and the consideration of a route that left us with means of escape should Dunkast have anyone even halfway competent planning this hunt once a trap gave away our location slowed us even further.

I have been hunted across rooftops before, of course. In Shaitush, in Pesh, more than once in Hain, where their Royal Guard have a peculiar lightfoot trick they do not teach to outsiders. The best sort of thievery is when they do not discover your presence until you are long gone, and what is assassination but a theft of life? I had no time to think, or I might have been reminded of a slippery plunging chase my first time in Hain before I had learned to cache armor and weapons or even paid my first tithe to the Thieves Guild. That, or a winter chase in Antai, when I had stolen the contract for a particular merchant lord's life from Smahua of the Snake Clan and led half of her ilk on a merry chase indeed across the city to the Red House.

I had needed the money, and Smahua was too slow. The end of that chase bore a fruit of tradewire and coin in a leather pack, and I had left half of it on the counter downstairs at the Crimson Hole with her name attached to it. I was not *greedy*. I thought, why not share?

Except she took it as an insult, half-noble merchant's daughter that she was. There are none so jealous of their position as those who feel themselves weak.

But I had other things to think upon that night. Halfway to the Keep, I viewed the deceptively dark street below and blew out between my teeth, wishing my ribs would stop aching. I shoved Janaire into the cover of a high-peaked windowledge and looked again while Atyarik, glowering, sank on his haunches and peered into his *adai's* face. Darik's was the far-vigil; he scanned the rooftops opposite, head upflung and the rest of him easy, his bow unlimbered and an arrow loosely nocked.

"Catch your breath," I told Janaire, though I was the one gasping. "What possessed you twain to come out tonight?"

"Tis a good thing we did," Atyarik replied, acidly. "They almost had you netted, *adai'sa*."

"Many thanks for your help." Darik, polite and formal, smoothing the folds of politeness as usual. "Was that a Skaialan bard I heard?"

"Yes, the Blacknose fellow. He insisted." Janaire

rubbed at her temples, delicately. Her skirts did not weigh her down much, but then, she had Atyarik to help her when they were cumbersome. "At least the little one is asleep."

"And Gavrin?" I coughed, rackingly, spat into the street below. It did not quite freeze in midair, but the cold was beginning to work its way in past the heart-thumping heat of battle and chase. The warming breath requires deep movement of air into your lungs, and I could not manage it. My ear-tips twitched, and my fingers were numb. High, brassy horns sounded to the south and west—the attackers'. The deeper, richer tones of the Kalburn horns from the barricades echoed in reply, defiance made music. I did not like it; the Ferulaine horns were sounding not where they had been at dusk.

Now why is that, Kaia?

"We left him speaking with the queen." Janaire's term for Emrath was respectful. No doubt they admired each other's dresses roundly. "They hold bards in much honor here."

"At least until she hears him sing about going to sea." I coughed again, spat. It tasted of blood, and that was a bad sign. "Listen. Two streets over—they are both narrow, Tyaanismir, you should manage them even with your *adai's* skirts to haul—and do you turn hard south, you will have a clear path to the Keep. There is a parallel higher, on the eastron side, D'ri will take that to cover you with his bow." I glanced at Darik, an indistinct shape in the dark. Only his eye-whites gleamed. "It is how we returned on the third night, *s'tarei'mi.*"

"Are you well?" Janaire leaned forward, peering at me. "You sound strange."

"I am almost too furious to speak without screaming," I informed all three of them. My harsh throat-cut whisper gave truth to the not-quite-lie. "You left the safety of the Keep, and you are both ill-fitted to rooftop warring."

"We saved *your* skin," she pointed out.

I changed to tradetongue; I could not bear to continue in G'mai. "And that is why I have not yet cuffed you both, like the disobedients you are." I shook my head, quelled the blood-tinged tickle in my throat. "Go. Now. I can hear them coming."

"Where will *you* be?" D'ri had enough presence of mind to ask. His hair was a wild mess and his ear-tips poked through; he had lost his head-covering.

"There is another parallel, lower, to the west. I shall take that road."

Perhaps he did not quite trust my plan. His hand braceleted my wrist, a spot of warmth in the deadly darkness. "Why?"

"'Tis easiest." *That* time, I lied. "And that will mean you have the high ground, with your bow." *That* was the truth, though only half of it.

"I sense them too," Janaire whispered. Her eyes had grown round, and her cheeks, unblackened by soot, were twin Moon-reflections upon the mirror of a calm lake. "How many of those awful things has he made?"

"More than one," I snapped. "*Move!*"

Thank the Moon, they did, even Darik, who vanished into the dark as if he was made of its fabric.

I half-straightened, listening. Yes, there it was. The soft, *wrong* footfalls, creatures too large for the way their boots landed cushioned and cat-quick, and the hideous black blankness spreading from them. An irregular semicircle, and to the northwest, a thick clot of darkness.

"Invisible bastards," I whispered, in the rough argot of a Shainakh army camp, its lilt returning to my tongue as if it had never left. "They hide behind a grassblade, and put their arrows through a coney's eye." It was the first thing Ammerdahl Rikyat had ever said to me, in a tent on the Danhai plains as he hunched over a map-table and eyed the new recruits. He had gazed at me—tall for a G'mai female but small among sellswords, point-eared, with a single hilt rising above my shoulder—and laughed, as if he could not believe the recruiting agents had sent him such fodder.

Darik had no way of knowing what the western route entailed. For he had not been dreaming of it, near-nightly, the way I had. I forced myself further upright, and set off in a silent lope instead of the mad whispering scramble of the other G'mai.

The dreams had served me well; I knew what would happen next. There was a graying in the east; we had cut our time too close, and with dawn would come the attack on the last of the barricades.

MAKE THE BAIT SWEETER

RUNNING. Rattling tiles underfoot, trusting to speed and skill to keep me upright since I had no concentration for clumsily using Power to boot-stick my feet. The slopes were easy, and I paced myself, one hand to my side where the pain had settled, the easy, ground-eating pace of a weary sellsword used to long marches. I could run forever in this manner upon flat ground; across the tiles I veered, half-drunkenly, until I came to a place I recognized from many nights' dreaming.

I let my foot slip sideways and slid down, hanging for a brief moment from a carved waterspout to channel rain or springmelt, its high horns and leering smile familiar. The drop wasn't bad, the jolt upon landing merely enough to rattle, wringing a harsh cawing from my throat. I hacked and spat blood again, then set off up the street.

They smelled distress, the way the great sharpfins native to the Lan'ai near Hain are said to. Some say it is blood from the wounded they scent, the way wolves or *coyik* in Pesh's Broken Hills are said to do. An *adai* in pain, Power flaring and fading through the fringes of her mental walls, was irresistible.

Or so I hoped. If the others were quick they would reach the Keep. Slowing pursuit was my task; I had played wounded coney before many a time on the Plains—always on a fast horse and with a full quiver, though. This time I had my *dotani*, my knives, soot smeared all over me, and my wits.

It would have to be enough.

The foul gloves were quick, brutal, and full of an alien will. But they were not very *intelligent*. They dropped behind me, soft plops of diseased, half-melted ice. Stagger-stumbling, letting my boots catch upon cobbles, I *felt* the other G'mai as a sellsword hears distant music from the street while she rests across an inn-bed. Still moving, and the nasty, bruise-dark stormclouds behind them had paused. The foul gloves were everywhere, and now I realized Dunkast had merely been biding his time, waiting for Rainak Redfist's witchery-friends to come across one of his traps. Once *we* were dealt with, his Black Brothers would have an easier time attacking the Keep itself. Dunkast's *tain* and his allied bastard clans were expendable, the foul gloves were his true weapon, brought out into the cold to deal with an unforeseen foe.

Along with that Pensari gem, of course. It was a ruthless move, and one I might have admired if I were hearing this as a tale from afar, perhaps sung by a competent lutebanger. Dunkast was moving swiftly to remove an impediment, which meant he judged us —and Redfist—to be quite a stumbling-block. Now he must guess Emrath had been working against him; stupid of her, to wait for spring, but insurrection takes its own time. No doubt she had laid her plans as well as circumstances would allow, like the weaver she was.

Ahead, the street took a sharp turn to run true

northwest. I slowed, hoping to make the bait even sweeter. At least D'ri had taken his part without question. If he had not...

No. He will be safe, and when you reach the end, he will be there with his bow, and—

My left knee, much abused, buckled. I staggered, truly this time instead of an acrobat's play, and my belly-muscles twitched. Perhaps the man's kick had unmoored something vital. It did not matter, all I must do was delay them a little longer. My chin jerked up as if I had been struck. I leaned forward and began to lope again, that steady pace I am so familiar with. Tha-thump, tha-thump, the foot strikes and the body pushes itself forward while the rhythm burrows into brain and heart and bone. Horses are expensive, and a young sellsword—or one the dice have been unkind to—must depend upon her own boots to carry her to fresh starting in a new city.

Kalburn Keep reared before me, much closer now. There was a final barricade, a jumble of broken waggonry, other smashed lumber, chunks of masonry, iron spars for bracing, and behind it, torchlight glimmering. I had no breath to ask the guards to hold their bolts and flung myself at it, my left boot hitting stone, up, my right hand closing about a spar, and on the other side, a short drop, the cobbles jarring knees, hips, shoulders, driving my recalcitrant body forward like an old bent Pesh woman as my belly spasmed.

The shadows had changed while I coney-led my pursuers; from the battlements, an onlooker would see a line of grey in the east, a thin thread of crimson heralding a bloody dawn. It was still night in the shadows of overhanging buildings, stone faces frowning as a tired, limping sellsword halted in the clear space and whirled, her *dotani* glittering as it whipped free. Kalburn held its breath. The Black Brothers dropped from rooftop and loped up the cobbled street, slower now with their prey cornered.

They had been busy while we went to the Market, indeed. The barricade was still intact; they had dropped *behind* it, and with no G'mai *adai* to fling Power or bard to exhort the defenders, they found the frozen guards easy enough to dispatch.

Brought to bay at last, I exhaled smoothly, rolled my shoulders to settle them, and drew my largest knife. The dream rose under my skin again, except in it, I had not been this weary.

Weary or not, I knew what I must do.

They melded into the spatters of uncertain torch-light. Two, three, four. More behind me, now kicking and tearing at the barricade with heavy gauntleted hands. A flat shine to their deepwyrm eyes, and their furs hung flapping on gaunt-wasted frames. *That* was interesting, but with the ones behind me closing in, I had little time to wonder.

I charged. Not straight for them, though that would have been satisfying, but to the left, where the shadows were deepest. Boots stamping, my legs com-plaining, ice underfoot and my left knee threatening to buckle again before silence descended—it was not the killing snow-quiet I had discovered after my mother's death but the white-hot clarity of battler-age. There is a moment, when the body has been pushed past endurance and your enemies are still all about you, when the last reserves inside a sellsword —those crockery jars full of burn-the-mouth, sweet-heavy *turit* jam—are smashed. Muscle may pull from bone, bone itself may break, but the sellsword will not feel it for hours. The Shainakh call it *nahrappan*, the Hain a term that has to do with a cornered ani-mal, and in G'mai it is called the *s'tarei's* last kiss, and it is said that even after an *adai*'s death a *s'tarei* may perform one last action, laying waste to his opponents.

The Skaialan call it *berserk*, and there are tales of their warriors fighting naked except for crimson chalk-paint, touched by Kroth's heavy hand and driven mad.

Pain vanished. My *dotani* clove frozen air with its familiar sweet sound, blurring in a low arc as I turned sideways, skipping from cobble to cobble with no grace but a great deal of speed. The far-left Black Brother had an axe, and all remaining thought left me as it moved, hefted as if it weighed less than a straw. Their soft, collective grasping burned away, I left the ground and *flew*, turning at the last moment, the arc halting and cutting down, sinking through fur and leather, snap-grinding on bone, and the Black Brother's mouth opened wet-loose as his arm separated, neatly cloven. The axe, its momentum inescapable, sheared to the side, and since his left hand was the brace for the haft it arced neatly into his next-door compatriot, sinking in with the heavy sound of well-seasoned wood.

Their child-high screams rose but I was already past, and Mother *Moon*, I longed to turn back. The burning in my veins, the sweet-hot rage, *demanded* it.

Instead, I put my head down and bolted. Thump-thud, thump-thud, the street familiar now, each shadow turning bright-sharp as my pupils swelled, the taste in my mouth sour copper and *katai* candy, a mix that meant I was tasting blood and remnants of my body's last reserves. Kalburn Keep loomed ever closer, a great frowning block of stone, and if I could reach the end there was a narrow housefront with a door left deliberately unlocked to the right. Once inside, I could be up the stairs and out a high window, onto the roof-road again, up and down while the foul glove-net closed upon empty air. There was an easy way into the Keep from there, if D'ri had reached it and secured the knotted rope—

Whistle-crunch. Another high childlike cry behind me as a heavy black-fletched arrow, its curve aimed high and sharp to give added force as it fell, pierced a pursuer's skull, shattering it in a spray of bone and grey matter.

Kaia! Thin and very far away, struggling to reach me through the rage. *Kaia, down!*

But my feet did not tangle together, and I did not fall. Fleet as a deer, the *berserk* upon me, I was an arrow aimed high as well. The dream turned to a soap-bubble swirling for a fallwater's drain; a giant, painless impact slammed into my back.

It was a crossbow quarrel, and its head punched through the right side of my ribs, crunching bone and spearing lung-tissue. It still did not hurt; beyond pain, I was still running when the darkness took me, and the guttural scream of a *s'tarei* echoed against ice-rimed cobbles.

In the distance, spilling from the hills into the cupped palm of Kalburn, came the plaintive baying of horns.

COMMON KNOWLEDGE

THE GREY IN THE EAST, shot through with gold, became a smear of blood. Smoke from the burning of Kalburn veiled the new morning, ice-vapor rising in thin curls over road, forest, shattered houses...and a mass of Skaialan upon torkascruagh, *a wedge driving across the north to break the Ferulaine supply lines.*

Emrath Needleslay, as soon as she received word Rainak Redfist had been sighted in Karnagh, had sent messages to every clan. By the time she walked the Connaight Crae to the Standing Stones, those who could not stomach more of Dunkast Ferulaine's witchery and high-handedness were well upon their way, and the summons, echoing through smaller Stones in every village and town with columns of pink phosphorescence, merely quickened their pace. Riding through the drifts, braving the cold just before the deepcrack-freeze when trees in the deepest forests sometimes explode as their sap turns to ice all at once, the Highlands rose against the Ferulaine.

Banners snapped and fluttered upon cold, smoke-freighted wind, and the bastard clans poured from the city's gates to meet the challenge. But they were weary from the cold and sleepless nights spent wondering if the ghosts of Kalburn would choose their bolthole to strike next, and their lord's most fearsome warriors were deep in the choke-tangled streets of the Old City chasing a tired, wounded foreign sellsword. By the time the Black Brothers heeded their master's silent call, the bastard clans had been broken between the hammer of the fullborn and the anvil of Kalburn's ancient walls.

No quarter was given, and those who had wished for a seat at the great clan-tables died in the snows. The siege of Kalburn was broken; the Needleslay rode from her Keep upon an albino torkascruagh with Rainak Redfist upon a black one at her side, and none dared call him a kinslayer. Now it was common knowledge that the accusation had been groundless, now it was held to be self-evident that he, and no other, was the Connaight Crae.

I heard of this later, of course. I lay, fever-wracked, on a narrow pallet buried in the earth-heated depths of the Keep, as Gavridar Janaire sought to hold me, and my s'tarei, to life.

Dunkast Ferulaine's baggage train was taken, and there was much rejoicing over the chests of pale gold stamped with wolf's head.

∼

THE SORCERER HIMSELF was nowhere to be found.

SINK ALONE

I passed in and out of a deep, thundering red-black cloud. Lightning was white bone, pain-paths sparking, Power coruscating through the halls of a ruined keep. My chest was a cracked egg, a riven stone, a shattered helm.

"...lucky," someone said, in sharp, clear, sweet G'-mai. "On the other side, she would be gone."

"It hurts." A ragged inhale. I knew *this* voice. It was Darik, and I felt only a weary relief that he was alive before pulse and breath both halted. The cloud turned deep and thick as the Pesh alcoholic syrup that passes for wine, toothrot-sweet and capable of inducing vomit if not heavily watered. They drink it straight, but a foreigner, not acclimated, does not dare.

I lifted *out* of myself, a bird with white wings and a blood-dripping beak freed from its carrion kill at last.

CLASH OF STEEL, *the battle yell caroming and sliding between my dry lips, the screams and howls of the wounded.*

Rik's face, glazed with blood and battle-fury. "Fall back! Get back, woman! Fall back!"

The horrible whistling sound, Rik's agonized scream as the quarrel buried itself in his chest. I screamed with him, grabbed his surcoat, and dragged him backward as four more crossbow bolts whistled through the air, thocking solidly down in blood-soaked earth.

He had taken the quarrel for me.

"Leave. . .me!" Blood striped his lips, he spoke under a chaos of sudden screaming. "That's an. . .order, Kaia!"

"Like hell I will!" I screamed, dragging him with hysterical strength, my boots slipping in blood-mired earth, grass trampled, the ululating yells of the tribesmen growing ever closer as I dropped him and drew my bow. The Danhai would not take either of us today.

Not if I could gainsay them. I nocked the first arrow, my dotani quivering in the earth where I'd driven it; the standard of my division-of-one. "No." Through gritted teeth, drawing back the bow as the shapes became visible through the smoke, my jaw aching with tension, "I shall not leave you, Ammerdahl Rikyat, ordered or not. You owe me at dice."

Then the first rider, yelling as he bore down on us at a gallop, longsword out. The arrow, released and whistling, bow sounding thrice more before I had to drop it and grab my dotani, because though I'd killed four of them there were six left, they were too close and I had nothing but my sword and my fury to protect the man lying wounded behind me.

It would have to be enough.

I HAD CARRIED Rikyat through the mud and blood to the healers's tent. Now I knew what it felt like, each step a grinding, driving the bolt in deeper. One quarrel for him, another for me. Was it luck, or a balancing of a merchant's scale after I left him to die?

My luck will turn against me, Kaia!

Then he should not have betrayed me. And yet, I felt only weary unsurprise.

You cannot escape what you are. I had fought it, but in the end, I had chosen my life and my temper, and paid for both.

"*No!*" Janaire yelled, in knife-sharp G'mai. "*Breathe, you ungrateful bitch! Breathe!*"

Convulsing, blood and lung-fluid spuming from my lips, racked on a cold pallet, and the pain, Mother Moon the *agony*, a spear in my chest turning, turning, grinding, splinters drawn free of the wound and blood welling, Power biting at torn flesh and knitting lung, windpipe, bone, and pain-path together, muscle twitching and sealing itself against invasion, skin pulled free and flapping grotesquely before melded to flesh underneath. It was cold, and it *hurt*, another fountain of fluid choked from mouth and nose, stinging.

I could not be dead. It hurt too badly.

More Power, forcing bone to regrow at many times its usual pace, a deep stabbing restless ache as if I were a stripling again with the stretching pains. My ribs creaked like trees under a heavy wind, and the noises I made were a whipped animal's hopeless pleading. I did not care if I died, as long as the pain stopped.

It did not stop. It went on, and on, and on, and each time I screamed another voice rose with mine, hopeless and hoarse. They say sharing halves a sorrow, but there was no halving this bloody, foaming, sharptooth sea.

Finally, the waves of grinding, furious black pain became a little smaller, more evenly spaced. They receded, leaving me gasping down frigid, knifelike air, and the oppressive weight of Power—two *s'tarei* and a fully trained *adai* spending force recklessly—slid away, too.

Kaia. Ragged at the edges, a single word I no longer knew the meaning of. Something behind me, propping me up. Arms around me, and a soft damp warmth against my hair was a mouth that for a moment, I thought was my own. My chest ached, abraded from within and without, and another sea rose to swamp me. This one was dark and cold, and I crawled into its embrace gratefully.

And yet, even then, I did not sink alone.

NOT TODAY

IT WAS A SEVENDAY, all told, of Gavridar Janaire at my side night and day, Darik holding me to life as I convulsed, Atyarik feeding Janaire all the Power he could reach, and Gavrin and Diyan running to fetch bandages, dried herbs, great steaming mugs of sofin, vast platters of food both D'ri and Atyarik plunged into to gain energy for their physical frames, both feeding Janaire vital force as she, in the deathly dream of a healer working at full gallop, plunged her hands into my chest and forced flesh, bone, and nerve-strings to reknit themselves.

Redfist took his turn with bringing the food, stood by the door with his big hands dangling and his hair loosed from its club. After the third day, he appeared with smears of their crimson chalk-paint upon his cheekbones, as is the custom with a Ska-ialan with kin at death's door or just past it. They hold weeping in some disdain; the paint—they call it *wohedlach*—is their open mark of rage or grief. The men paint themselves for battle, and the women for childbirth or when those children have met some misfortune.

When my body could breathe without Janaire's

constant prompting, when the danger of infection from bolt-splinters drawn from the gaping wound was past, and when I lay in the lethargic trance of the newly healed, Atyarik carried Janaire to the room given to their use and they both collapsed to sleep for a day, a night, and another day. Propped upon Darik in a small *skauna* room heated by fitful earthfires, his knees on either side of me, my back to his chest, inclined so my lungs would not fill afresh with fluid, I lay as if dead.

On the seventh day, I stirred. There was a glaring pink scar piercing my right breast, and its companion on my back among other marks of battle twitched as my breathing deepened. Bandages crusted with dried blood and lungfluid crackled when I shifted. My right side cramped in slow waves, muscles protesting both over-activity and forced rest. My fingers began to twitch, then my toes. A close, stale, damp warmth filled this tiny room—a *skauna*, the benches removed and a pallet set against the far back corner. Someone was breathing into my hair, slow regular swells, and my eyelids were almost glued shut. A single candle, lit a half-mark ago, burned in another corner, shielded by a bowl-glass bell.

I longed for a bath. For *chaabi* and flatbread. For a session with Ch'li the iron-fingered in Hain, her hands kneading the aches out of every muscle. For a pot of mead, or even *haka*, and a game of nothing more interesting or dangerous than Festival dice.

Darik did not move as I slithered from his arms. Deeply asleep, his head tilted back and his mouth slightly open, his cheekbones standing starkly out and his hair still Anjalismir-trimmed, he was the picture of a battle-weary *s'tarei*. Blood—*my* blood—soaked his clothes, and I winced. I could not smell the room because my nose was, like my eyes, full of crusted matter, and for that I was grateful.

At least I had not soiled myself. *Empty is the way to wholeness*, some Hain swordsmen say, but it is also the way to make certain your trews will not be full should night-hunting or rooftop-running end badly.

The stone floor felt wonderfully cool against my overheated palms. I half crawled, half dragged myself closer to the candle in its glass belly-home, craving light. My legs would not quite work properly, and my knees felt as bruised as the rest of me. I propped myself against the wall and stared at the candle, lifting my hands and examining them when I could find the will to do so.

Calluses from daily practice, thin white knife-scars, my nails trimmed or bitten short. Dirt and dried blood grimed into the creases, the lines Pesh fortune tellers with strings of glittering sequins over their faces claim to read. It took several moments of rest before I could scrub at my face with both palms. The rents in my sherte and jerkin flapped loosely; I was wasted as a dreamweed-chewer.

Healers say the body knows what to do, they merely aid its natural yearning to wholeness. I tweezed aside torn cloth, touched the scar bisecting my right breast, its nipple slightly oval now instead of round. A pang shot through me, the body remembering. I did not think Skaialan healers skilled enough to deal with such a thing. No, only a Haiian or a G'mai *adai* could possibly have performed such a feat, and even then, not with certainty.

Was it lucky that Janaire and Atyarik had followed, or not? I rested my head against the stone wall and looked at Darik. We are bred to the twinning, we G'mai, and do not survive its breaking. And yet, perhaps one of his will could? Would it have left him free of the burden of a flawed *adai*?

At least if I had died I would not be called upon to *respond* to this. It was one thing, to carry a fellow sell-sword to the healers' tents after he had taken a crossbow quarrel for me.

It was *quite* another to have Janaire save my own life.

I sat in that tiny stone cube, sweating and shivering, my braids half-undone and my skin crawling as I shook like a *vavir* addict denied the weed. For the first time in a very long while—many a season indeed—I had no idea what I should do next. The silence was all around me, *inside* me, even the small sound of the candleflame swallowed by a cold far deeper than any even the Highlands could produce. My hands turned into fists. The back of my head met the stone, softly at first, then with more force. Even *that* produced no noise, just a strange soft sensation down my aching back, briefly halting at the unseen scar where the crossbow quarrel had first met my skin.

A faint gleam showed under Darik's eyelids. His arms twitched, tensed, and he lunged fully into consciousness and up into a fighting crouch at the same moment. He reached for a hilt, but his hand closed on empty air.

I knew the feeling. My ribs flickered, lungs laboring though I was doing nothing but *sitting*, and the candleflame in its protective carapace shuddered. Everything flickered, but when the world steadied I found D'ri's forehead against mine as he crouched before me, his hands warm and familiar around my own, sour breath mingling with mine and the cold cracked in half, falling away in useless sheets and scarves.

"All is well," he repeated, softly. "All is well, Kaialitaa, little sharpness."

I found my voice, hoarse and cracked but still mine. "The others?" A clot in my throat, I coughed to expel it, could not even spit. "Janaire? Atyarik? Diyan?"

"All well. The siege is broken, the freeze is upon us, there is nothing to do but wait."

That was welcome news. And yet, it did not comfort me. "Wait?"

"Yes." He leaned forward, his hands tensing, biting mine. "Atyarik blames himself, the minstrel is long-faced, the barbarian quarrels with the queen here daily. His temper is almost as short as yours." He was hoarse too, a painful scraping. Screaming in tandem with your *adai* will break even the deepest voice, I suppose. "The Gavridar courted mind-scarring, but is resting comfortably."

I winced, wished again I could spit. The mass in my throat was uncomfortable, to say the least. It reeked of copper, and its edges were suspiciously soft. "You are angry."

He did not bother to grace such an observation with a nod. "You are alive. It is enough." He drew away, rocking back upon his heels. His boots creaked, filthy with dry-caked roofdust.

I did not expect as much, certainly. "Is it?" The dream had changed, left me witless and gasping, a fish pulled to shore.

"How could it not be?" He lifted my dirty hands, examined them minutely. I tried to pull away, but he did not let me and I was weak as a newborn. "I have made a vow, *adai'mi.*"

"A vow?" I repeated his inflection, too. Soft, precise, informative. It almost hurt to hear him speak in such a manner.

"I have sworn, upon your name, to hunt down this *Ferulaine*." A foreign word in the middle of G'-mai, and his tone made it a curse. "I will take his head, Kaia. That should please you."

"What would please me is a bath," I whispered. "And some chai, and us safe in some other place than this. Darik…"

"I do not care for my *own* life, Kaia, but *yours* I will not be careless of." He pressed his lips to my knuckles, hot shame flooding me.

I could not tell if it was mine, or his. "Careless is not the word for you," I managed. The cold silence had left me, and for once, I was glad of its absence instead of craving its clarity.

"One day I shall ask you what the word is." He let go, and stood, a little more slowly than usual. At least my own physical weariness blunted my feeling of *his*. "But not today."

"D'ri—"

But he was already stalking for the door. I slumped against the wall, and began the laborious process of trying to haul myself upright.

I could not. I could only rest against the stone, hearing his ruined voice echo in the hall as he demanded food, fresh clothing, and oil for his *adai*.

CLIMB TO ME

My legs were tremble-weak as a new colt's, and threatened to spill me sideways each time I gained some approximation of standing. Redfist, with his smeared cheeks, carried me up stone stairs to the half-familiar room Darik and I shared, our gear piled in the corner and the window well-shuttered. I could not even *clean* myself, D'ri had to attend me in a *skauna*. I am not given much to embarrassment, but having to be set upon a privy like a child near induced a measure of blushing. Afterward, Darik vanished to attend to his own cleansing, and probably some manner of fresh nourishment.

Tucked under a heavy weight of blankets, I stared at dark ceiling beams and white plaster, listening to blackrock and wood burn in the wide fireplace. Footsteps and voices in the hall outside kept me clinging to wakefulness; that, and the gnawing under my ribs despite all the sweetened porridge and sofin I could keep in my shrunken stomach.

When the door opened, after a brief token rap, I expected one of the G'mai. Instead, it was Gavrin, a lumpish brown woolen hat clamped over his shag-lengthening hair and his half-Pesh complexion turned ruddy by the chill. He carried a Skaialan git-tern, a fine instrument of mellow inlaid wood glowing with several applications of rosy varnish. His boots were new, too, and deep with plush fur. He even looked a bit taller, and broader in the shoulder.

The North agreed with him, apparently. The only thing missing was his usual shy smile, or the small duck of his head when his gaze met mine. He settled in the rude chair next to the bedside, the gittern held close, and began the process of tuning it. His hands, too large and raw-looking for anything else, became fluid and graceful with strings and pegs underneath them.

The fire crackled. I tried to summon a smile. None came. "Another sea-ballad?" I croaked. *Mother Moon, save us all from such torment.*

He shook his head, the ear-flaps of his new cap moving uneasily. His throat-apple bobbed as he swallowed. Gavrin plucked at the strings, a liquid stream echoing in the dark well of the gittern's belly. It was a plaintive tune, the thumping rhythm of Skaialan reels slowed and set sideways until muted and mournful.

Then, our lutebanger began to sing in Pesh, the long-crying, moaning tongue of his childhood, and I stiffened in my bed.

He sang of Kaia Steelflower, within who lay a true heart that would give all she had for a friend. *That* helped me smile, a pained grimace. If this got out, I would have no end of castaways and limpets clogging my keel.

Then the rhythm changed, and his voice dropped, slowing even more into a lament. Kaia Steelflower, he sang, who came to her friends' aid despite heat, ice, dust, assassins, or witchery...and was the loneliest of all beings, because she walked ever alone.

I sagged against the mattress, the pillows, and

stared. The fire pop-crackled, working into the rhythm of his strumming, and I flushed hot, then cold. Had I my strength, perhaps I would have risen, taken the gittern from him, and stove in its belly as my own had been crushed by Dunkast's foul gloves. And cast it into the fireplace, as well.

Pesh is an unlovely language, but somehow he made it match each note, dropping into harmony where another singer might have taken an easy thread. Singing in tradetongue required flexibility, this required...something else. He was at his best, our lutebanger, when he made the instrument of his mother-tongue work against itself and the melody besides.

Ever, ever, alone, the refrain echoed, *ever and always alone, for I come to my friends, but I do not let them climb to me.*

He did not look at me; Gavrin gazed instead at the shuttered window. Mirrorlight described his cheekbones, touched his mouth and his quivering throat as he held the notes, and he must have been listening to Janaire's humming of G'mai counting-songs, for there was a familiar pattern behind the words. The chorus repeated, twice, and each time the scar on my chest ached, a strip of fire matching blackrock's deep secretive fire.

Finally, his fingers limped on the strings, and the song turned harsh. Blood on ice, a crimson rose, and the words spiraled to their conclusion.

It is lonely in the snows, he sang. *So lonely...* The harmony resolved, the final line spilling like snowmelt through numb fingers.

I will come if you call, but I will not let you climb to me.

He held the last syllable for a short while. When it failed, for his throat seemed somewhat full, he laid

his hand flat upon the strings, stopping the reso-
nance. Gavrin did not look at me. He simply stood,
cradled the gittern, blinked a few times against the
swelling salt in his eyes, and left, closing the door
gently upon an invalid.

I lay rock-still, beam-straight, fist-clenched, and
too weak to rise or to call out. The Yada'Adais,
teachers of Power among the G'mai, can drive a point
home with a single look, an inflection, a syllable. The
Hain fighting-masters use a blow or a parable,
thieves everywhere a knife and sharp sarcasm.

Now, I discovered, a half-Pesh lutebanger could
do it with a song.

DEEPCRACK FREEZE

SMOKE ROSE from the scars of Kalburn still, the entire city under a thin grey pall as the sky cleared and temperatures plummeted afresh. I pushed the woolen baffles aside and peered between shutter-slats and the layer of ice upon glass. The Keep rose high above a white blanket cupped in the valley-palm, and the distant mountains looked near enough to reach in a day's ride, the space between their knife-edge and the eye turned crystalline. The slice of the Old City I could gaze upon showed little damage, and the broad backs of *torkascruagh* flooded it once a day, driven to the Great Market to cleanse its expanse.

Did they smell my blood upon the cobbles? They were fat and sleek despite the cold, those tusked creatures, for the battle-dead vanish into their maws. Kroth's elder brother, the trickster Ferran, sometimes appears in their stories as a hefty, red-eyed *torkascruagh* with golden testicles, attended by his *wal'kir* as they cleansed the battlefield. *Sick-eaters*, the Skaialan call them. To fall in combat and be consumed is an honor to them, though a Shainakh, with their corporeal afterlife, would shudder at the notion.

Only the Black Brothers were not granted the

mercy of cleansing. Their headless bodies, stinking and running with blackened juice, hung from the Old Wall, suspended from gibbets and thus dishonored.

"You shall catch cold," Janaire said, softly, in respectful G'mai. She sat near the fire, frowning slightly as she plied her needle upon black cloth— one of Atyarik's shertes, mending with quick, delicate stitches. Her braids, looped over her ears, were decorous and glossy, and she looked little the worse for wear except for the shadows under her dark eyes.

She would not accept my thanks, but she spent her time in the room, mending or repairing gear, occasionally chiding me to stay in bed or eat more heavy, greasy Northern food. Darik arrived at nightfall to relieve her watch, and I did not ask how he spent his days, for the cold hung upon him, and the smell of effort. Sparring outside with the Skaialan warriors did not dull the rage in him.

I would have found his silence uncomfortable, if it had not been so similar to my own. He spoke upon nothing but commonplaces, and I…

I longed for my *dotani*. Or my knives. The floor was bruising cold, but I stretched every candlemark, loath to lose flexibility. Janaire had wrought well; the scar did not pain me. I was simply weak, and the thin daylight brought inside by mirrors, bright enough to sting the eyes, paled in comparison to the world outside the window.

"I shall not," I murmured. "It would ruin your fine work."

Not a day trudged through its endless, tooth-gritting candlemarks that I did not make some reference to my debt. She accepted with a nod each time, the graceful politeness of an *adai*. This time, however, she looked up from her needle-wielding. "You do not have to keep thanking me, Anjalismir Kaia. The deed is its own reward."

"A sellsword pays what is owed." The proverb had no sting in G'mai, especially with my inflection so honorific. I scratched under my braids, loose and looped to keep the mass of hair from tangling as I lay abed.

"Mh." A noncommittal noise, and she returned to her sewing.

It irked me. What did she seek to prove? Gavrin's refrain echoed in my head. I knew my temper was none too sweet, and the rest of me followed suit. Why did they attach themselves to me, if I was so terrible? Of course, Janaire and Atyarik were not attached to *my* sherte-strings. It was Darik they followed, their princeling wandering far afield. And I had not *asked* the minstrel to come along. Diyan... well, the Vulfentown wharf-rat knew a steady meal and a lack of brutality was worth a great deal along the Lan'ai Shairukh coast. Redfist, of course, knew the value of a blade.

Were they friends if I was merely useful?

A knock at the door was too blunt to be a G'mai, and too definite to be Gavrin. Redfist swept the heavy lumber wide, Diyan bouncing in past him, and my relief was short-lived, for the boy's wrist was wrapped in a bandage and Redfist looked grave and glowering.

"What happened?" Of course I barked the word, as if we were upon a Shainakh training-ground.

"Oh, *cha*, just a rikky-spit." The boy grinned, shaking a fringe of dark hair from his broadening face. "Dree teachin me sword, says I'm too old but he do a mun fae o'it." He was too old to begin G'mai training, of course, but soon he would be large enough for a longer blade.

"Come, let me take a look." Janaire rose, and soon enough was fussing over the injured wrist while Diyan grinned hugely. Ignored again, I returned my gaze to the window.

Redfist bent to peer past my ear, out the shutter. He smelled of the *skauna*'s heavy oil, and fresh outside air as well. "There's to be a Council called," he murmured, passing news as one does along a line of ranked blades, with the mouth hardly moving. "Such a thing has not happened for many a year."

I let the baffle fall, closing us back in a mirror-lit cave, and half-turned. "Is there doubt over what course to pursue?"

"Nay." He stood too close, but the healthy heat-haze from him was welcome. "'Tis all but agreed. It waits only upon ye being well enough to attend, K'ai."

"I see." I did not take the step away that would have removed me from his radiating heat. "You wish an ally present."

"Oh, I've plenty allies, lass, especially now. What I wish is a *friend* there, to watch me back."

My cheeks turned to flame, and I had to breathe out, steadily. Had Gavrin sung to them? They did not know Pesh, of course, but...he could well explain.

The fire made a crackling, comforting noise. "The swelling is not bad," Janaire said softly. "You'll mend."

"Much thanks, lady." The urchin swept her a bow, its lightness showing D'ri had, indeed, been teaching him how to move. "Tarik and Dree bringing up dinner. Say it's not your'n, but will do."

"And Gavrin?" she inquired.

As if summoned, the lutebanger appeared, knocking twice at the door and sliding inside, smoothing his shapeless hat and brightening at the sight of Janaire. I turned back to the baffled window, studying the nap of figured cloth. Who had woven this pattern, I wondered?

"Ye're quiet, K'ai." Redfist, his thumbs in his belt, loomed where he had planted his boots. I could not decide if his sheer size was comforting, or if I felt as a sapling in the shadow of a much larger tree with matted, reddish branches. "Does yer wound pain ye, then?"

"Not much." The...discomfort...lay elsewhere. I told my knees they would have to wait to loosen, and they obeyed grudgingly. "How long does the treecrack last?"

"A moonturn, perhaps a tenday after that." A single, mountainous shrug. He was still in a *kelta*, but at least he'd combed his beard. "Hard to tell. Ferran rules it, and he is a bastard."

I attempted levity. "Does your Dunkast pray to him?"

"Looks like he prays to none but his own bloody self." Redfist glanced aside, a bright blue flash. We shared the look of two old sellswords hearing campaign news, and judging whether or not our own skins would be pierced in the meanwhile.

It was pleasant to find something still familiar, in this new world I found myself inhabiting.

In short order, Darik and Atyarik arrived, the latter bearing Janaire's *tavar'adai* so she could dine as a traveling *adai*, in comfort. Behind them were servants loaded down with more, and it seemed they were determined to eat here.

I pushed the cloth aside again. Redfist said no more, and moved away. Rooftops below, smoke and the busy scurrying of those whose work it was to build, repair, feed, clothe.

My only trade was the sword, and it does nothing but kill. And you do not accumulate trade-siblings like a merchant, or favored customers like a courtesan or innkeeper. It is not a life meant for *building*, whether physically or...otherwise.

Certainly you could sing with fellow irregulars, dice with them, spar and curse at or fish them out of mud-holes, laugh at their jests or bloody their noses when they made one witticism too many. But precious few of them are *friends*. Even fewer will stand between you and a bolt, or play wounded-coney to buy you time to retreat, sacrificing their own chance at escape.

Even those who did might turn on you later, when one of their gods whisper-burned in their fevered heads, or simply because if there was one constancy in the world, it was that people, of whatever land, clawed to their own advantage. The rarity was those who did not.

I will not let you climb to me. Would it be better, I wondered, if I could craft of song of my own, to tell Gavrin it was not that I did not wish to?

That it was simply, merely, I did not know *how?*

I was the one ever climbing, and the end was never reached. Easier to keep a shield-wall of distance, and retreat, seeking only companions who could not wound me.

If you do not care, they may harm only your body, not the rest of you.

There was quiet laughter behind me, and the good smell of heavy fare. Their shared circle of dinner was warm, and complete, and utterly closed to me. I was ravenous, but I lingered at my post, watching the sudden winter night fall from the mountains across the Old City. Kalburn was full to bursting, the Keep storehouses flung open to feed those who had come from every corner of the Highlands to shake off a false king's yoke. The treecrack freeze gripped firm, and fatal.

When it ended, the hunting of Ferulaine would begin.

TO BE CONTINUED...

GLOSSARY

Several languages are represented, among them G'mai, Shainakh, Skaialan, trade-pidgin, Antaiin, Hain, and Clau.

A'vai – Again.

A-thatch, thatch'n – Displeased, insulted, angered but not to the point of blows

Adai – Female G'mai

Adai'in – good instinct

Adai'mi/sa – My *adai*/Lady *adai* (honorific)

Adarikaan – shining blade

Adjii – Adjutant

Albestrkha – alabaster

Alhaia – Clau greeting

Baia – pungent plant/herb; "poor man's woundheal"

Bakaii – illicit lover

Ban'sidha prutaugh – ill-tempered whore

Boydhar – a species of bird

Cha – (Pidgin.) Expletive, inquiry, agreement, spare syllable.

Chaabi – Clau stew

Chedgrass – tall grass found in streams, silky with plump, pearl–like seeds

Cor'jhan – suitor/betrothed

Dauk'qua'adaia – Everstars (guide with constant light), guiding s'tarei to adai

Dauq'adai – Seeker

Dhabri – head-covering, headwrap

Dolquieua – green rot, "the eating moss"

Donjon – jail

Dotanii – long and slightly curved, slashing blades with oddly shaped hilts meeting the hand differently than other blades

Fallwater – shower

Farrat – A ferret-like creature, but more closely related to cat than weasel

Fatan'adai – telling the future

Fuchtar – a common expletive

Fislaine – an herb, pungent smell

Haigradabh – An ancient word left over from the Darjani tongue, meaning something like laughter

Haka – strong, clear liquor

Hamarai – wall of silence

Hamashaikhan – The Shainakh Emperor's Elect

Hath'ar lak – The sleep after a battle, also, a gift from a kindly grandmother or a quiet death in bed surrounded by relatives

I'yah'adai – Literally, "power-exhausted"

Ilel'adai – vision

In'sh'ai – G'mai greeting or word of thanks

Insh'tai'adai, s'tarei, ai – "As the adai (wishes), the s'tarei (performs)."

Jada'adai – Twinsickness

K'wahana – type of Clau bird

K'yaihai – G'mai womanhood ceremony

Kaahai – Bitch, female donkey, balky mare

Kadai a'adai allai – G'mai battle–cry

Kafa'adai – A G'mai scribe

Kair'la – The same verb for sweet syrup-crystals dissolving in water, with insanity tacked onto the end.

Kimiri – type of cheese

Kiyan – Silver piece

Lahai'arak – a complex mess of a battle, no victory for either side

Lya-ini – G'mai, honorific for "agemate (of my cohort)"

Malende – bad spirits

Navthen – a chemical inside a clay ball that produces a hot burst of flame when mixed with ortrox that coats the outside.

Piri-splitter cut – sword technique

Qu'anart – smoked fish or mutton stew

Rako – forest creature with a black mask and a striped tail

Rheldakh – a Pesh bird-goddess, known to give succor to travelers

S'tarei – male G'mai

S'tarei'mi/sa – My s'tarei / Sir

S'tatadai – a marshcat, a taller G'mai female

Sadaru – ritual suicide

Sh'yada'adai – the testing of a young adai's Power

Sharauq'allallai – outcaste, murderers, kinslayers; those the G'mai cast away

Shaurauq'g'd'ia - a foul emission from the loins of a diseased demon

Skai'atair - unclean, foul, outcaste, the dregs of a poisoned bowl, as well as assassin

Stilette – a thin, sometimes flexible blade

Strinlin – instrument

Sunbrollaugh – patricide

T'adai assai – "It is done."

Taih'adai – "Starseed" a teaching sphere

Tamadine – a particular unit of soldiers

Tannocks – idiots

Taran'adai – Speak-within (telepathy)

Tavar'adai – A combination chest/fireside seat for an adai's comfort while traveling

Tsaoganhi – A wandering people, much given to singing and mending

Vavir – a drug made from the *vavir* weed

Ya'hana – Tracks, tracking, a mark in snow, the bending of a blade of grass

Yada'adai's'ina – Literally, "student teacher"

Yada'Adais – G'mai teacher

Zaradai – witchlight

ACKNOWLEDGMENTS

Thanks must go to Skyla Dawn Cameron and Mel Sanders; I wouldn't have written Kaia's further adventures without their encouragement. A great debt of gratitude is also due you, my faithful Readers.

Let me thank you once again in the way we both like best, by telling you a story...

ABOUT THE AUTHOR

Lilith Saintcrow lives in Vancouver, WA, with her children and a house full of strays. You can find more of her books at www.lilithsaintcrow.com.

ALSO BY LILITH SAINTCROW

Steelflower

Steelflower at Sea

…and many, many more.

CPSIA information can be obtained
at www.ICGtesting.com
Printed in the USA
BVHW080358140122
626128BV00006B/84